Naples to Northanger

Being, chiefly, extracts from the correspondence between Eleanor, Viscountess Hapworth (née Tilney), and Miss Catherine Morland

Ronald McGowan

Copyright © 2016 Author Ronald McGowan

All rights reserved.

ISBN: 978-1-326-75331-3

DEDICATION

To Derek and Julie, and everyone else who voted "Remain", in the hope that this continental farrago will be some small diversion from the woes of Brexit.

CONTENTS

LETTER THE FIRST: MR HENRY TILNEY TO VISCOUNTESS HAPWORTH, IN PARIS   2

LETTER THE SECOND: VISCOUNTESS HAPWORTH TO MR HENRY TILNEY   6

LETTER THE THIRD: VISCOUNTESS HAPWORTH TO MISS MORLAND   8

LETTER THE FOURTH: MISS MORLAND TO VISCOUNTESS HAPWORTH, IN PARIS   13

LETTER THE FIFTH : LADY HAPWORTH TO MISS MORLAND   17

LETTER THE SIXTH : MISS MORLAND TO LADY HAPWORTH, IN PARIS   24

LETTER THE SEVENTH : LADY HAPWORTH TO MISS MORLAND   27

LETTER THE EIGHTH : MISS MORLAND TO LADY HAPWORTH, IN PARIS   36

LETTER THE NINTH : LADY HAPWORTH TO MR HENRY TILNEY   39

LETTER THE TENTH :   LADY HAPWORTH TO MISS MORLAND   41

PARIS   41

LETTER THE ELEVENTH :   MR HENRY TILNEY TO LADY HAPWORTH, IN PARIS   48

LETTER THE TWELFTH :   MISS MORLAND TO LADY HAPWORTH, IN PARIS   50

LETTER THE THIRTEENTH :   LADY HAPWORTH TO MISS MORLAND   55

LETTER THE FOURTEENTH :   LADY HAPWORTH TO MISS MORLAND   64

LETTER THE FIFTEENTH :   LADY HAPWORTH TO MISS MORLAND   70

LETTER THE SIXTEENTH :   MISS MORLAND TO LADY HAPWORTH, IN GENOA   80

LETTER THE SEVENTEENTH :   LADY HAPWORTH TO MISS MORLAND   86

LETTER THE EIGHTEENTH : LADY HAPWORTH TO MISS MORLAND   90

LETTER THE NINETEENTH : LADY HAPWORTH TO MISS MORLAND   GENOA

LETTER THE TWENTIETH : MISS MORLAND TO LADY HAPWORTH, IN GENOA   **115**

LETTER THE TWENTY-FIRST : LADY HAPWORTH TO MISS MORLAND   **118**

LETTER THE TWENTY-SECOND : MISS MORLAND TO LADY HAPWORTH, IN FLORENCE   **133**

LETTER THE TWENTY-THIRD : LADY HAPWORTH TO MISS MORLAND   **137**

LETTER THE TWENTY-FOURTH : MISS MORLAND TO LADY HAPWORTH, IN FLORENCE   **141**

LETTER THE TWENTY-FIFTH : LADY HAPWORTH TO MISS MORLAND   **144**

LETTER THE TWENTY-SIXTH : VISCOUNT HAPWORTH TO MR HENRY TILNEY   **148**

LETTER THE TWENTY-SEVENTH : MR HENRY TILNEY TO LORD HAPWORTH, IN ROME   **151**

LETTER THE TWENTY-EIGHTH : MR HENRY TILNEY TO LADY HAPWORTH, IN ROME   **153**

LETTER THE TWENTY-NINTH : MISS MORLAND TO LADY HAPWORTH, IN ROME   **155**

LETTER THE THIRTIETH : LADY HAPWORTH TO

MISS MORLAND   158

LETTER THE THIRTY-FIRST :   LADY HAPWORTH TO
MR HENRY TILNEY   161

LETTER THE THIRTY-SECOND : MR HENRY TILNEY
TO LADY HAPWORTH, IN ROME   163

LETTER THE THIRTY-THIRD : LADY HAPWORTH TO
MISS MORLAND   165

LETTER THE THIRTY-FOURTH : MISS MORLAND TO
LADY HAPWORTH, IN NAPLES   167

LETTER THE THIRTY-FIFTH : LADY HAPWORTH TO
MISS MORLAND   169

LETTER THE THIRTY-SIXTH :   MISS MORLAND TO
LADY HAPWORTH, IN NAPLES 182

LETTER THE THIRTY-SEVENTH :   LADY HAPWORTH
TO MISS MORLAND   184

LETTER THE THIRTY-EIGHTH :   LADY HAPWORTH
TO MISS MORLAND   186

LETTER THE THIRTY-NINTH :   MISS MORLAND TO
LADY HAPWORTH, IN PALERMO   190

LETTER THE FORTIETH :   MISS THORPE TO MISS
MORLAND   192

LETTER THE FORTY-FIRST : MISS MORLAND TO MISS THORPE, IN PALERMO 194

LETTER THE FORTY-SECOND : MISS MORLAND TO VISCOUNT HAPWORTH, IN PALERMO 195

LETTER THE FORTY-THIRD : MISS MORLAND TO LADY HAPWORTH, IN PALERMO 197

LETTER THE FORTY-FOURTH : LORD HAPWORTH TO MISS MORLAND 199

LETTER THE FORTY-FIFTH : LADY HAPWORTH TO MISS MORLAND 200

LETTER THE FORTY-SIXTH : MISS MORLAND TO LADY HAPWORTH, IN PALERMO 206

LETTER THE FORTY-SEVENTH : LADY HAPWORTH TO MISS MORLAND 208

LETTER THE FORTY-EIGHTH : MR HENRY TILNEY TO LADY HAPWORTH, AT BRISTOL 211

LETTER THE FORTY-NINTH : MRS HENRY TILNEY TO CAPTAIN TILNEY 213

LETTER THE FIFTIETH : LADY HAPWORTH TO CAPTAIN TILNEY 214

Other books by Ronald McGowan

Jane Austen "Amplifications"

Pride Unprejudiced

The Journal of Miss Jane Fairfax

Colonel Brandon's Secret

Mansfield Restored

To Make Sport for our Neighbours

Others

The Golden Apple

What I did in My Holidays

Letter the First: Mr Henry Tilney to Viscountess Hapworth, in Paris

Northanger Abbey

1 November 1802

My very dear Eleanor,

I trust that your ladyship will permit such a familiar form of address from a mere commoner, though he is your brother? We shall else soon become mired and lost in such a spate of "my ladys", and "your ladyships", and "my lady viscountesses" that any kind of sensible correspondence will be well nigh prohibited. If, however, such liberties offend your ladyship's exalted sensibility, pray tell me now, and you shall hereafter have more than enough of such condiments for your taste.

All of us here at Northanger are longing to hear how you have progressed since leaving us, and hoping that you are now safely settled in Paris for the winter, for, surely, you will not venture to cross the Alps into Italy at the worst time of the year.

Catherine particularly asks me to enquire of the latest fashions in Paris, both in dress and in literature, for her tastes in both owe much to you.

Yes, Miss Morland, though not yet physically present, is now included in "all of us here at Northanger", and I am even permitted to refer to her by her Christian name! The plea you made for her – and for me – at the last moment before you left with your new husband has so worked upon our father that at last he has given his consent, and we are only awaiting your return –and Charles's, of course – for the next wedding to take place.

But, pray, do not hurry back on that account. I intend to make the most of my last days of bachelor freedom, and you must do the same with every day of your honeymoon.

I could not wait to tell you my news, and now I cannot wait to hear yours. What an impatient, tiresome elder brother I am become! But I would take it very kindly if you would write, now and then, to Catherine. She has very grateful memories of you, and wishes very much to be friends once more with her future sister. At present her manner of correspondence, as far as I have had opportunity of judging, appears to me to be the usual style of letter-writing among women, that is to say that it is faultless, except in three particulars.

"And what are they?" I can hear you ask, even from the far side of the channel.

I am sure that you are perfectly aware, dear sister, that they are a general deficiency of subject, a total inattention to stops, and a very frequent ignorance of grammar. I am perfectly sure that you are also aware that these observations do not apply in any way, shape or form to your own, excellent style, which I hope will serve as an ideal model for Miss Morland.

But, however, if I may for just one moment venture to be serious, Catherine would love to hear from you. She has always valued your friendship, and has missed it sorely during these late days of estrangement between Northanger and Woodston. Now that our father can no longer forbid it, few things would give her greater pleasure than to resume your former intimacy. And, of course, if you write to her, I shall still hear all your news, but will be saved the trouble of replying. What could be better?

No doubt you will be spending as much time at

the couturiers as at the art galleries, and we look forward to hearing about them both. But, pray, have a care when selecting fabrics, for I fear you have no-one around you with a thorough understanding of muslin.

Very soon, however, I am convinced that your knowledge will even surpass that of

Your loving brother,

Henry.

Letter the Second: **Viscountess Hapworth to**
Mr Henry Tilney

Paris

5th November 1802

My dear Brother,

You may address me as "your supreme exalted highness" if it please you. It will be no more nonsense than the rest of your missive, for I know better than to expect any sense, in the normal course of things, from you, when you sit down to pen and paper. I met a "supreme exalted highness" the other day, and should be very sorry to consider myself in any way his inferior. He was quite as foolish by nature as you often are by design, dear brother, the heir to some pinprick German principality, and perfectly incapable of tying his own shoelaces or telling you what day it is, but insistent on every last syllable of his titles. Since they were in High Dutch, I leave it to you to calculate the exact number of those syllables.

I am well, and have taken note of what you have to say in your last letter. I trust that the adequacy of my grammar will serve, along with the sufficiency of full stops, to excuse the total absence of subject.

That absence I intend to remedy in my next letter, which shall, as you suggest, be addressed to Miss Morland. She, I beg leave to assume, will take more interest in the continuance of a correspondence, and find it less arduous an undertaking, than a mere brother would. I send her no compliments, nor no congratulations with this sheet, as I intend to fill several more to send to her direct.

For what else do we females have to do?

This particular one, at any rate, has found quite a sufficiency, of ways in which to occupy her time lately, but for details you will perforce have to wait for Miss Morland's narration of those scraps she chooses to dole out from what has been passed on to her by

Your loving sister,

Eleanor.

Letter the Third: Viscountess Hapworth to Miss Morland

Paris

5th November 1802

Dear Miss Morland,

Permit me to say how glad I was to hear from my brother in his latest letter that my father has finally given his consent to you and Henry marrying. Just before our departure I made one last appeal to him, and rather hoped that he might be persuaded by the pleas of a viscountess where those of a mere daughter had been of no avail, for it was evident to all that never had the general loved his daughter so well in all her hours of companionship, utility, and patient endurance as when he first hailed her "Your Ladyship". That this might induce in him a state of such complaisancy as to wish all about him happy also was my earnest desire. It had not yet been fulfilled when I took my leave of Northanger, and the news that at last we all have leave to be joyful has been all that I could desire to make my honeymoon perfect.

Until Henry wrote to me, however, I could not be sure, but now that I am, you may be sure, too, my dear Catherine, that the prospect of such a sister to come home to was all that was wanting to make my happiness perfect and complete.

You were not at the wedding, I know, my father still continuing in his obduracy at that time. This itself was a source of sorrow to me, as I had wished for you for my maid of honour. But you will forgive me, I know, if I confess that I had so many other sources of happiness on that day that even your absence could not mar it.

We shall spend many long hours discussing it when I return to Northanger- that and the prospect of another such ceremony in which you will be even more intimately concerned.

But I cannot resist boasting of my beloved Charles, who I know will love you almost as much as I do, and whom I know you will love also. My husband is really deserving of me; independent of his peerage, his wealth, and his attachment, being to a precision the most charming young man in the world. Any further definition of his merits must be unnecessary; the most charming young man in the world is instantly before the imagination of us all. Concerning the one in question, therefore, I have only to add that this was the very gentleman whose negligent servant left behind him that collection of washing-bills, resulting from a long visit at Northanger, by which my own Catherine was involved in one of her most alarming adventures.

Do you remember that first night of yours at Northanger, my dear? I remember finding you the following morning in something of a state, occasioned by the discovery of a mysterious chest, crammed with arcane manuscripts.

Yes, those were my husband's washing bills you found in the cold light of day. He was plain Charles Covenham then, a country gentleman distantly related to nobility, and not nearly a grand enough match for the daughter of General Tilney. The series of unlikely chances by which he became the heir to the family estates and titles would have done justice to your Mrs Radcliffe, but you will forgive me if I postpone their relation until we are more comfortable.

I ought not to leave you in suspense like this, I know, but what I am really longing to hear is exactly how it has come about that we are shortly to be sisters, after these long months of waiting. I had quite become reconciled to waiting until there should be no father – on one side at least - to forbid the banns. But what a difference this will make, my dear.

When I left Northanger I had no notion of soon to be hearing such splendid news. My father seemed as obdurate as ever. He had, you recollect, refused you admittance to the ceremony, and for a while we were in fear that your absence would necessarily involve Henry's too. I know perfectly well to whose sweet, understanding nature I owe my brother's attendance on my wedding day, and you may believe me when I tell you that I intend to be forever grateful.

You may tell Henry that the description he gave me of foreign parts when he was trying to discourage my notion of honeymooning on the continent was perfectly accurate. Abroad *is* filthy, smelly, crawling with vermin and full of foreigners, many of whom are filthy, smelly and crawling with vermin themselves, especially the soldiers, of whom there seem to be an inordinate number at every street corner.

I will say no more, however, for I am perfectly

aware that this correspondence has been wished upon you by Henry to save himself the trouble of answering my letters (and also, I suspect, to enable him to reply quite truthfully that he has not heard from me should our father enquire), and I do not propose to trouble you further until I hear from you, in your own hand that such trouble would not be uncongenial to you.

    Until then, believe me to be

    Your sincere friend,

    Eleanor Hapworth.

Letter the Fourth: Miss Morland to Viscountess Hapworth, in Paris

Fullerton

12th November 1802

My Lady Viscountess,

Permit me to inform you of the delight with which I received your letter of the fifth November. It seems so strange that you should be in Paris, surrounded by Frenchmen, while we were standing around the bonfire burning Guy Fawkes. It is not so long ago, after all, that it was Boney that we were burning.

You are far too kind to write to me, and I am sure that you cannot really wish to spend time corresponding with an ignorant girl when you could be enjoying the famous delights of the French capital. I am sure there must be *some* delights to be had there, and they must be famous, for everyone seems to be talking about them just now, but I fear I have no real idea of what they may be. That just shows how ignorant I really am, of course, and you will be ashamed to continue in converse with me, but it must be so, for Henry says so. Most men, he says, look for complete imbecility in a wife, but he is perfectly content with mere ignorance.

I do my best not to be ignorant, I am sure. At least I know that Paris is in France, rather than France in Paris. But is it not all rather horrid there? Are the streets not red with the blood of aristos, with a guillotine on every corner? Do the *tricoteuses* sit in their doorways, singing the *Ça Ira*?

And what of the mobs of *sans-culottes*? They must be very frightening. I should be terrified every minute of my stay in such a place, and quite unable to venture onto the streets. You must be very brave.

But then you have a husband to protect you, which must be a source of such comfort. I have never met my lord your husband, but I am sure that he must be the most wonderful man in the universe, my own Henry excepted, of course. I cannot tell you how it makes me feel, to be able to write those words at last –"My own Henry." But you will feel the same about my lord Viscount, I make no doubt. I have never met him, but he must be very special to be worthy your love.

It must be wonderful to be married, I am sure. I

long for it every day. Henry tells me I must not urge you to return, and of course you must make the most of your time in such exciting places as you are due to visit, but, oh, how I long to see you again, and not just as matron of honour!

I am perfectly aware that I must not encroach too much upon your time, but it would be a joy to me if you could spare a moment now and again to send me just a line or two. The days pass so slowly at Fullerton, now, especially when Henry is at Woodston, where his duties take him far more often than I should like. As a clergyman's daughter myself I should appreciate his reasons, and I do, but that does not stop each minute of his absence languishing into an hour. And yet it is not so long ago that every day was too short! Now it is only the days when he is here that vanish in a flash, and every other is interminable.

You father has invited me to stay with him until you return, but I am sure that you will understand, and forgive me, if I tell you that the thought of his society, unassisted by yourself or Henry, does not inspire me with an irresistible urge to take up the invitation. My memories of Northanger Abbey are, to be sure, so mixed that I find myself sorely puzzled what to make of them.

But please do not think that I intend any criticism of your childhood home, nor of your father. I mean only that, without your presence there (and, preferably Henry's too) Northanger's attractions are outweighed by those of Fullerton. I make no mention of Woodston, as Henry has not taken me there yet, though he has promised I shall have the decorating of the parsonage to oversee soon.

But I fear I have already troubled your ladyship too much with my girlish ramblings, and can only beg your indulgence and repeat that the odd line in return would greatly please and gratify

Your Ladyship's most humble servant,

Catherine Morland

Letter the Fifth : Lady Hapworth to Miss Morland

Paris

18 November 1802

My dear Catherine,

I was very glad to receive your letter, although why I should be I am sure I do not know. With all those "My Lady Viscountesses", "My Lord Viscounts" "Your Ladyship's most humble servants" etc. one would think you were writing to a stranger rather than to an old and dear friend who is soon to be your sister.

As your sister, I must insist. We are "Eleanor" and "Catherine" to each other, or we are nothing. Please expunge these odious honorifics from all future correspondence, or I fear that future may be all too short. If we two cannot write freely to each other, with whom can we do so?

Now, let us have a comfortable coze, my dear.

You ask about the delights of Paris and the perils of its streets. Both of these, I fear, are much the same as in London. But that will mean very little to you, who have never been to London, and I only mention it to show that I am become quite

Cosmopolitan. But, as to Paris, imagine a larger Bath, dirtier, much more squalid, much less airy, but every bit as crowded. Imagine every member of that crowd conversing incessantly, not in the genteel murmur of the Englishman, but at the very top of his voice, and in a dozen different languages. Imagine all that twice over, and it will give you something of an idea of a quiet day on the streets of Paris.

You are not mistaken in supposing that it must be quite horrid here, but not, I think, in the sense you use. Bloodstains are no more in evidence than on the streets of Bath, the *tricoteuses* have all gone home, and I am ashamed to confess that I have yet to see a guillotine. As for the *sans-culottes*, with their Phrygian caps and their pitchforks and scythes, I fear they are all gone home too. What is horrid is the dirt everywhere, and the smells, and the people's manners, or rather lack of them. And there are soldiers everywhere, constantly demanding *papiers*, and money, too, if they can induce you to hand it over.

Fortunately, we are staying at the embassy, so we are spared the worst of it all.

Yes, I have seen the site of the Bastille, at

which I defy even you to shudder nowadays. It is nothing but an open space, much needed in that part of the city, I may assure you, surrounded by tenements, with a few stones jumbled here and there. The old castle, at which no doubt you would shudder, was torn down very shortly after it was stormed by the mob. Street vendors there will willingly offer to sell you a 'stone from the Bastille' at a very negotiable price, but Charles tells me that there are enough of these stones on the market to build all of Paris, let alone the notorious prison. There is talk of erecting some sort of monument there to the "glorious revolution", but I have seen nothing more solid than talk as yet.

Monsieur Frenchman, as far as I have seen, is much given to talk about "gloire", among other topics, but not much given to doing more than talk. He is also much given to celebrating, in extravagant phrases, the peace between our two nations, which would be a great thing, could one but trust in such protestations. Here is the first verse of a song I heard sung in the street the other day, which will give you the flavour.

"Anglais, Français, restez unis,

Qu'à vos chants l'univers réponde:

Quand de tels rivaux sont amis,

Qui peut trembler la paix du monde."

    There was much more of the same sort of thing, but I will not trouble you with the rest. It is all nonsense, of course, for all that it is true enough, as far as it goes, but it all rests on the third line. We have all been brought up to hate a Frenchman, and I dare say they reciprocate. So many lives have been lost, on both sides that I cannot think they will be soon forgotten. We have met here with a great deal of surface charm- the French are very good at that, of course – but very little of what I should consider to be sincere friendship, or even open intercourse. The French, of a certain class, that is, always seem to be looking over their shoulders, aware that an informer could be listening, or an *agent de police* taking notes. One can hardly blame them, of course. They have lived with these things for ten years, and do not expect any great alleviation of their lot, even now.

The lower classes love our money, certainly. The perfidious English gold about which Bonaparte rants so much is very well seen by the shopkeepers, even more so than their own Louis d'or, which one now has to be careful to call Napoleons. I remember an acquaintance once describing London as "a place where anything can be had, for money", and the same is true of Paris, to the ultimate degree. Without money to bribe the necessary officials it is impossible for an Englishwoman even to obtain permission to walk the streets. With money, anything can be had, including the incarceration of one's rivals or enemies, on any charge or none. *La grande nation* this may be, but never think they are the same as us. They behave differently, they act differently, they think differently. The sheer foreignness of everything can be overwhelming at times.

But forgive me, my dear, this letter has turned into something of a political tract. I should say that I have been listening too much to Charles, were such a thing not patently impossible.

My first impressions of France, were, I own, almost overwhelming. The ragged rabble on the quayside, shouting and gesticulating in a way that quite alarmed the returning emigrés on our vessel, stretched out dirty, civil hands to help the English milords down the landing ladders and carry their bags to the waiting inn. The street scenes en route to our lodging were a revelation. Instead of the villainous sans-culottes and blood-stained scenes of Mr Gilray's cartoons, everywhere we found friendly faces and orderly citizens. The women in their red camlet jackets and high aprons, the long, flying lappets to their caps, the wooden sabots with scarlet tufts that clattered perpetually on the cobbles, the sound of all the world talking at once, the tang of garlic, smell of coffee, boiled milk and crisp rolls were all delightful to the senses at first. With use, they quickly became tedious, however. I confess that, fearing an umitigated diet of snails and frogs, I had secreted a home-cured ham among my baggage, for emergencies, but have so far had no occasion to resort to it. The new France, indeed, lives far better than we could have expected, provided one has money, of course. That is what all the smiles are for, after all.

I am sorry to disappoint you with my prosaic nature. I am sure that you could find much to shudder delightfully at in Paris. There is no shortage of desecrated convents with gaping roofs, flapping hangings, torn up vaults, deserted palaces lapsing into squalid decay and weedy royal gardens. There are even guillotines, with their slanting blades and gaping wicker baskets to be seen here and there, for those that way inclined. I confess myself not greatly tempted, however.

To do the place justice, there is also a great deal of splendour among all this decay. The shops I will leave for another day, but Charles's old aunt, who we met here, and who remembers Versailles in the old days, declared she had never seen such magnificence as in the First Consul's apartments in the Tuileries. I have not seen them myself yet, so I will refrain from comment.

We go to the opera tonight, to see The Mysteries of Isis, which has been recommended to us by Lord Cornwallis. I promise to devote my next letter to as minute a description of the evening as if it were an assembly at Bath or a dinner at Northanger.

Until then, my dear, believe me to be

Your loving soon-to-be sister,

Eleanor Hapworth.

Letter the Sixth :   **Miss Morland to Lady Hapworth, in Paris**

Fullerton

22nd November 1802

Dear Eleanor,

I cannot thank you enough for all the trouble you have taken over your reply to my letter. It really is too good of you to spare the time.

Things are very dull here at Fullerton, but when have they not been so? Your adventures in that well-known haunt of Jacobins and revolutionaries are all that keep us entertained when Henry is not here.

Do, please, take no risks. I mentioned to Mrs Allen the other day that you were in Paris, and she was quite shocked.

"I have the fondest recollections of Miss Tilney," she said, "and should hate to hear of her having to flee for her life from the sort of mobs they have in those parts. It must be terribly wearing, never knowing when your head is going to end up on a pike. How would one have one's hair dressed for that, I wonder? I should not like to be in her shoes, my dear."

But however, she sends her compliments and kindest regards, and begs to know the latest fashions, especially as regards muslin and long sleeves.

Sally is of quite another opinion, and never tires of saying how much she would like to go to Paris, and what a jolly adventure it would be.

I think you must be very brave, as well as clever, and wise, but I have always thought so, and such a nature is only to be expected of Henry's sister. You have been kind enough to say that you are my sister, too. How I long for the day when that will be strictly true!

Residing, as you do now, in such a big and important city, I expect you do not notice the winter drawing in so much as we do in the country. The roads between here and Northanger have been very difficult these past weeks, and I cannot help wondering how much longer Henry will be able to keep making his regular visits. Without his arrival to look forward to every week, I do not know what I should do.

But mention of Henry reminds me that I have been very remiss in not giving you news of him before now. He is well, and full of plans for our wedding, and sends his best love. He never fails to ask for your latest news when he comes to visit, though I fear I have had very little to pass on to him so far.

I am so longing to hear about your night at the opera. I have never heard an opera, still less seen one, as we were not so fortunate as to attend one when I was at Bath with Mr and Mrs Allen. All I know of them is Doctor Johnson's definition – "an exotic and irrational entertainment." I imagine one must needs be very learned to understand them, since they are all in Italian, but you are so clever that I am sure that does not signify to you in any way.

I cannot tell you how pleased and proud I am that you are so good as to write to me as often as you do, and hope that you will continue so to delight

Your very dear friend,

Catherine Morland

Letter the Seventh : Lady Hapworth to Miss Morland

Paris

29 November 1802

Dear Catherine,

I take your hint, my dear, and shall make an effort to write more often. I make no excuses for my past offences, which have arisen entirely from sloth, dilatoriness and procrastination.

Procrastination has been somewhat a feature of our lives here in Paris lately. We did not go to the opera the night I last wrote to you. How that came about is something of a tale in itself.

I will save that tale, however for another time, as you are so eager to hear about the opera. It will in any case sit better with a disquisition upon the Paris Fashions, about which at the moment I will do no more than tantalise you with the observation that they present a very broad range at present. The first Consul, they say, is somewhat of a puritan in regard to ladies' dress, and is planning to impose more severe modes. In the meantime the most extreme designs abound.

But, to return to your "exotic and irrational entertainment," we did manage to take our seats there the following night. The seats themselves were no great shakes. The Opera –or to give it its formal name, L'Académie Royale de la Musique, is at present performing from temporary accommodation in the old Théâtre Montansier on Rue Richelieu. It is said to be the largest hall in the city, accommodating seventeen hundred spectators. It may well do so, but only at the cost of being cramped, stuffy and very badly lit. The corridors and aisles are so narrow that one can barely squeeze through them, and, once in the auditorium, the views of the stage are so restricted that scarcely anyone can see more than half. In spite of all this, they tell me that it is always full.

For those who could see it, however, the *mis en scène* was certainly exotic enough, being set in ancient Egypt, with such lavish and impressive sets and costumes as – so they say- have never been seen on stage before. They were certainly extravagant enough, and definitely created an impression. Whether that impression was quite what was intended, I hesitate to say. Charles, who is a stickler for these things, and was in Egypt himself not so long ago, tells me that neither sets nor costumes bore any resemblance to the real thing, either of the present day or of three thousand years ago. The audience, however cheered them with the vehemence with which the Parisians reserve for those they either love or hate.

So much for the exotic nature of the entertainment. The French, of course, are mad about Egypt just now, and have been ever since Bonaparte's campaigns there. This, I conjecture, must be the irrational element in the performance, since one would have thought that any reminder of that campaign, so disastrous for them, would not meet with the best of receptions. Not so, however. Baron Denon's book has sold out at all the booksellers, *modes à l'Egyptienne* are everywhere, there is a Rue du Caïre, a Foire du Caïre, a Passage du Foire du Caïre, an enclosed corridor between two streets full of draper's shops selling oriental silks and such stuffs, where one may shop without any fear of the weather, and everywhere one sees *les vêtements Égyptiens, La Cuisine Égyptienne, le Café Égyptien* and so on.

Mais, pour tourner à nos moutons, as they say around here, what of the entertainment itself? You need not have feared for your Italian, my dear, since it was all in French, *Les Mystères d'Isis.* I never quite made out where Isis came in, and Charles tells me it was full of references to Freemasonry. Exactly what those references were he was unable to elucidate, since he is not one himself, and everything about them is secret, so that even if he was one, he would not be allowed to tell me. Freemasonry is a power in the land in France, in fact on the continent generally. One sees their grandiose lodges everywhere, and they are widely held to be behind every plot and intrigue that comes to light. This, of course, is common knowledge. Whether it is also true, I cannot venture an opinion.

The plot was quite exotic enough, too, with its mysterious powers wielded by the male and female protagonists and its interlocking love stories. The credit for its composition was given to a Herr Lachnith, from Prague, but from the very first notes of the overture I thought there was something familiar about it, and when the comic attendant came in with his whistles, I at last recognized the birdcatcher *Papageno* from *The Magic Flute,* here transformed into a shepherd named *Bochoris.* I had seen the real thing in London last season, and could not praise Herr Mozart's invention in it enough. This mockery of an adaptation, with all the best (for which read, hardest to sing) bits left out and replaced by patches from here there and everywhere (I am sure I recognized an aria from Titus at one point) quite spoilt the evening for me, until I gave up trying to follow the French and merely listened to the music, the power of which nothing can entirely subdue.

This was difficult enough under the circumstances. I caught myself about to write "You know what is like at the opera", but, of course, you do not. What it is like at the opera is that a large part of the audience go there for the purpose of seeing, being seen, and meeting their acquaintance, rather than from any desire - or even intention - of witnessing the performance, and refuse to let the music interrupt or otherwise interfere with their conversation. Those who do attend to the performance make very sure that their delight- or otherwise- is very publicly known, and the constant cheering, hooting, hissing, cries of "Bravo" etc. make for a very long evening. An evening at any sort of theatre in Paris tends to be spoilt by this sort of thing. The dancing at the theatres is wonderful – and the French do like their dancing, even in the middle of an opera – but the effect tends to be ruined by slovenly fellows, auditors who smoke and spit all the time, and fail to offer their seats to ladies. I should not like to venture to one of them unescorted.

The Parisians love the piece, however. It has been in performance, at one place or another, for some twelve months now, and the houses are always full.

This sentiment is not universally shared. We went on to M. de Talleyrand's afterwards. He has promised us some assistance with the passports we need for our journey onwards into Italy. Nothing can be done in France without the right piece of paper, and the man to go to for it, if you do not have the ear of the First Consul himself, is Talleyrand.

His reputation, I know, is not of the best. I have heard Lord Whitworth, in an unguarded moment, describe him as pompous, affected, insolent; a shameless liar with a diseased white face hanging like a decaying corpse over the top of his gaudy uniform: a trickster whose deformed feet are as crooked as his principles. This was in the course of a discussion of the list of demands Charles had brought from London for him to make to the French

Government after their seizure of Switzerland, and the reports we have from Naples that they are surveying the Adriatic Coast from Ancona to Taranto, and his excellency was perhaps a little heated. I do not profess to have Lord Whitworth's familiarity with M. De Talleyrand, but he can certainly charm when he wants to, and I have always found him polite and helpful.

I mentioned where we had come from and he remarked,

"Ah, *Les Misères d'Ici*! Quelle parodie d'un vrai génie. Je l'abomine, ça."

He went on to call it a wretched hotch-potch (un fatras pitoyable) and quoted a critic on the day after the first performance, who wrote that "In this wise, two beggars in filthy rags came masquerading before the public in the rich robes of the kings of harmony; and, in this sordid fashion, a true man of genius, disguised as a monkey, decked in flimsy tinsel, mutilated and deformed, was presented to the French people, by their tormentors, and the public was deceived."

Can you think of a single minister in England

who would show such emotion about what is only a public entertainment? Charles says that it is all part of Bonaparte's system. He has adopted from the Romans not only his title of Consul, but also their policy *of panem et circenses,* bread and circuses to keep the mob happy. The thought of the mob being kept happy by opera made me laugh at first, but Charles pointed out that the cheapest seats cost only fifty centimes, and that the theatres are filled with the lowest classes as well as the highest. This is deliberately so, he says, not merely to keep them off the streets, but also to keep them under observation. The ushers who show you to your seat – and woe betide you if you attempt to make your own way – are all in the pay of the Government, he says, and report everything they see and hear to the police.

He may be right, although he does tend to see spies around every corner, and I live in hope of catching him looking under the bed at night. I mentioned, jokingly, to Monsieur de Talleyrand that I had heard that every third Parisian was a government spy, and asked him if it was true.

He merely shrugged, and replied, with that crooked smile of his that one can never quite trust,

"La Vérité, milady 'Apvort' ? Qu'est que c'est?"

He did not go on to wash his hands after such a question, but I imagine his smile was much like Pontius Pilate's. To tell the truth (whatever that is), he rarely does wash his hands, or any other part of his body, nor most of his countrymen neither. Both sexes use a great deal of perfume, but it cannot quite make up for the prevailing odour.

But I fear I have delighted you too long with my disconnected musings on Parisian entertainment. Send me some good, honest English news in exchange, I beg of you, about something wholesome, like the apple harvest, or making your Christmas puddings. They say that travel broadens the mind, but there are times when I think quite the opposite is the case.

Let me hear from you soon and let a breath of fresh, English air into the smoky, French salons currently occupied by

Your affectionate friend,

Eleanor.

Letter the Eighth : Hapworth, in Paris   **Miss Morland to Lady Fullerton**

5th December 1802

Dear Eleanor,

How lovely to hear from you again, although your last letter made me feel even more ignorant than ever.

You write as if you are quite a habituée of theatres and opera houses, as I make no doubt you are, and you are not merely familiar with such establishments but you can actually remember the music you have heard in them, and recognize one opera from another. I fear for how I will show in Henry's company since he is used to such an intelligent and accomplished companion as you. I believe I heard some of Mozart's quartettos played while we were in Bath, but I fear we only had Purcell and Arne at home, and I was never much good at them on our old spinet. Can you recommend me a short, easy piece that I could learn to impress Henry with? It would have to be easy for me to learn it, and it would have to be short because I fear I could not afford a long one. I suppose I shall have to send to London for it, in any case.

You still make Paris seem quite horrid, with spies on every corner, and having to look under the bed at night to make sure there are no interlopers there. I am sure I should not like it, any more than you do. It must be awful to have to wait so long for news of home!

Does Henry really never write to you? Nor your father? You must forgive me if I tell you that I am not sure I should like to receive a letter from General Tilney. I am still quite afraid of him, you know. I cannot rid myself of the thought that any communication from him could only be to forbid the match once again. I am perfectly aware that Henry is far too good for me, and I cannot help remembering how kind and agreeable General Tilney was to me when we met in Bath, and when first I came to Northanger. And how all that changed at …. I was going to say, at a moment's notice, but it was actually with no notice at all. I spend at least part of every day in a positive terror that the next post will bring tidings of my dismissal, of the General's once more turning his face against us. He must meet with a dozen more eligible brides every day in London. It is foolish of me, I know, but now that our marriage has at last been acknowledged actually to be about to happen, I could not bear it if something went wrong again. Henry tells me that I must not fret so, and that to doubt the certainty of our marriage is to doubt him. I perfectly comprehend what he means, and I do not doubt him for a moment, but I cannot help being nervous. I own I am but a "*Wee, sleekit, cow'rin, tim'rous beastie*", as Mr Burns says. I cannot believe that I could be so fortunate, and never shall believe it until the ring is on my finger. What a happy day that will be, but never fear, my Eleanor, it shall not come until you do.

Until then, please write to me more often. Your letters are the greatest pleasure I have, from one end of the week, when Henry leaves, to the other, when he comes again. I do not mean to put you to any trouble, however, and wish you only to continue with correspondence that is congenial to you, and I will do everything I can to make sure that the most welcome you receive is that of

Your steadfast friend,

Catherine.

Letter the Ninth : Lady Hapworth to Mr Henry Tilney

Paris

8th December 1802

Dear Brother,

Would you be so sweetly kind as to hunt out the old sheet music for those Mozart piano sonatas we used to play, and the duets, too?

Then would you be even kinder and see that they are delivered to your Catherine in such a way that she does not know where they came from, nor who sent them?

She has asked me to recommend a few pieces she could learn to surprise you with, and sooner than put her to the expense- and suspense- of ordering things from London or Bristol, I thought of the old music room at Northanger. And while you are there it will do no harm at all if you pass the odd hour or two with our father, and keep him favourably disposed. He never liked your self-imposed exile to Woodston, you know, and would be overjoyed to see you again. Do not expect him to show it, however. Can the Ethiopian change his skin, or the leopard his spots?

It will rather spoil the surprise if Miss Morland discovers that the scores came from you, and to prevent that will cost you some little application, but I have full confidence in your ingenuity, and in your delight in exercising it.

You need not fear that this request will once more involve you in a protracted correspondence, but compliance with it will earn the sincere gratitude of

Your loving sister,

Eleanor

Letter the Tenth : Lady Hapworth to Miss Morland

> Paris
> 13th December 1802

Dear Catherine,

You must not be such a goose as to suppose that, after all, some horrid chance is set to prevent you from marrying my brother. Such things, it is true, do occasionally happen in real life, but not nearly so frequently as they do in your Gothick novels. Trust me, my dear, or, better still, trust Henry. Only an act of God could separate you now. Since you are a parson's daughter, I will not speculate upon how likely such an act may be. But no action of my father would suffice now, I am sure. Having once given his consent, he must now be honour-bound to stand by it, and should he now withdraw it, you and Henry would be perfectly justified in ignoring such a recantation, and proceeding with the ceremony without him. No-one has to give the *groom* away, after all. Although I have never met them, I am satisfied that your parents, who must be both kind and reasonable to have engendered such a daughter, would agree with me.

We are become so intimate that it seems strange that I have never met your family, and that Fullerton exists for me only in a kind of dream world as described by Henry and yourself. I assume that "Sally", whom you mention in your last letter but one, must be your sister. Is she all that a sister should be, a support and friend and confidante to you? I always wanted a sister –older or younger would have made no matter – to share secrets with, but it was not to be. Pray, tell me more about your family when next you write. Do you have other sisters? Do you have brothers? What kind of people are they all? Are they all sweet and kind like you? They, too, will be my family before too long.

It has been very dull and wet here lately, with nothing of consequence happening. Charles has been much closeted with the ambassador about our travels onward into Italy, and, of course, we have no real friends in Paris.

I finally got to see the pictures and statues at the Louvre yesterday, but I will save the full account for my next letter. I am conscious of being already somewhat behind with my news, having promised you particulars of the latest fashions and the story behind our missing the opera that first night we had designed to go there.

Since both these subjects are somehow related, I will deal with them now.

Paris is full of shops, selling everything that one could wish for, from marmalade and millinery to mummified marmosets, the last being much in demand for *décor à l'Égyptienne.* The great shops in the mansions of the former nobility are imposing enough, to be sure, but their very magnificence somehow lacks taste. They overdo their effort to impress. I could say more about this universal French tendency to over-egg the pudding, but I must stick to my theme for now. Everywhere there are tiny dressmakers shops, and miniscule milliners, so that one never has to walk far for a change of wardrobe.

I fear my powers are not adequate to describe the current fashions here in any manner that will be intelligible to those who have not seen them. To make up for this want in my ability, I enclose the plates from the latest *Journal des Dames et des Modes.* They will, I am sure, give you a much better idea than I ever could.

It is said that Bonaparte disapproves, and is attempting to enforce a new style of his own, but at present the prevailing style is still *à la grecque*, that is to say, in the Grecian mode. In Paris at least, the chemise is no longer worn, nor anything much else in the way of underwear, as far as one can see – and one can see quite a lot. The styles and cuts vary from those which leave very little to the imagination of the beholder to those which leave nothing at all. Henry would be in his element here, as the recognized expert upon muslin, since muslin is very much the favoured material. Mrs Allen, too, would be able to practice economy to her heart's content, since very few yards indeed are required for the latest creations.

One would think that, with so little outlay upon cloth to be considered, prices would be accordingly low, but I have not found that to be the case. The real advantage, however, is in the timing. Order a dress in England and you will have to wait two weeks. A Parisian seamstress will run one up for you, in the latest style, for the morrow, or the day after at the latest, with only one fitting at the very end.

I ordered just such a dress from Madame Chose round the corner, and wore it that first night we were intending to go to the Opera. At first all went just so, but when we were in the carriage and I removed my shawl, Charles's eyes almost popped out of his head.

"Eleanor!" he cried, "What *are* you wearing?"

"This is my new gown *à la mode de Paris*." I replied. "Do not you think it suits me?"

"But you cannot go out like that! It is not decent!"

"You seemed to find just such a dress more than acceptable the other day at the Tuileries Ball. Madame Recamier was wearing one just like it and you danced with her three times. And the First Consul's own sister wore one very similar, too. Indeed, this one is said to be modelled upon hers."

"Ma'mselle Pauline is a law unto herself, and even so her reputation is far from spotless. And as for Madame Recamier, she is Madame Recamier. She is not Milady Hapworth. There is nothing else for it. We shall have to go back for you to change. After all, it does not signify if we are late for the performance."

And before I could say another word he had leaned out of the side of the fiacre and instructed the driver to return.

It was only on the stairs up to our apartment that a thought came to me.

"Oh!" I exclaimed, "I told Suzette we should not be back until late and that she might visit her sister across the river. There will be no-one to help me out of my dress. You will have to do it for me."

"I told Pierrot much the same, only it was his widowed mother." Charles replied. "We shall have the apartment to ourselves."

"Then come help me undress, my love." I said.

I do not believe Charles had ever undressed anyone before. He made such heavy weather of it that by the time he had finished we had quite other things on our minds.

So the opera had to wait, and the dress never did get worn. I shall bring it back with me and you shall have it, my dear. We are much of a size, after all. It would be interesting to see its effect upon Henry. He is, after all, such a connoisseur of muslin.

I have just remembered that you asked me about music to play for Henry. Forgive me, my dear, the subject went quite out of my head. Let me think a while, and oblige

Your loving friend,

Eleanor.

Letter the Eleventh : Mr Henry Tilney to Lady Hapworth, in Paris

Woodston

16th December 1802

Dear Eleanor,

It is done. The package is gone to Fullerton, suitably disguised. There was a little problem, in that one of the sheets bore notes in a certain person's hand that might have been recognized, as might the hand of the covering note, had I not taken precautions.

But I think I have fudged it all nicely, and the deception will take. I look forward to being delightfully surprised in due course.

The best surprise would be to hear that you and Charles were on the way back. Then we could really get down to preparations for the main event.

But do not curtail your inspection of ruins and

galleries on my account. Who knows how long the opportunity will last. From all one reads in the newspapers, this time next year the Channel may well be blockaded again.

Let us hope that before then we shall have the happy event of your return, and the still happier one that waits upon it.

The times grow ominous again. Take great care of yourself, and none at all for

Your timorous brother,

Henry.

Letter the Twelfth : Miss Morland to Lady Hapworth, in Paris

Fullerton

21st December 1802

My dear Eleanor,

How like you it was to take such trouble after I asked you about music I could learn for Henry! When I did so, the very most I hoped for was a few scraps of information. I had no notion that you would write to your old music teacher and ask him to send me these beautiful scores. You must have been a far more conscientious pupil than I ever was, as one of them, I see, has notes upon it in your own hand, which serves to make it all the dearer to me.

I never thought to put you to so much trouble, nor, indeed, to Signor Arrigo, who has hurt his hand, poor man, and had to pen the covering note with his left hand. It must be such a trouble to a musician to have injured a hand. Pray give the gentleman my thanks too.

But how sly of you to have pretended to have forgotten! I was taken quite unawares, and Sally took great delight in quizzing me upon the mystery parcel.

It is so good in you to take an interest in my family, too. You must know that my father is a clergyman, without being either neglected, or poor, and a very respectable man, though his name is Richard, and he has never been what is commonly called handsome. He has a considerable independence besides two good livings, and you know quite well that he is not in the least addicted to locking up his daughters. My mother is –and it is just as well, I suppose, since her eldest daughter is quite the opposite - a woman of useful plain sense, with a good temper, and, what is more remarkable, with a good constitution. She had three sons before I was born; and instead of dying in bringing me into the world, as anybody might expect, she still lived on-- lived to have six children more--to see them growing up around her, and to enjoy excellent health herself. A family of ten children will be always called a fine family, where there are heads and arms and legs enough for the number; but the Morlands have little other right to the word, for we are in general very plain and stupid.

My mother it was who wished me to learn music; and I was sure I should like it, for I was very fond of tinkling the keys of the old forlorn spinnet; so, at eight years old I began. I learnt a year, and could not bear it; and my mother, who does not insist on her daughters being accomplished in spite of incapacity or distaste, allowed me to leave off. The day which dismissed the music-master, I am ashamed to confess, was one of the happiest of my life up to then. I have mended a little since, especially since I met you and Henry, and become quite proficient in my old age. On a good day, I can rattle off *"London Bridge is Falling Down"* and *"Pop goes the Weasel"* with the best of them.

With nine brothers and sisters to describe, you will scarcely expect, I am sure, the expenditure of ink and paper that a full description would entail. You have already met James, of course, and must have your opinion of him and of his solid worth.

Sally, or rather Sarah (for what young lady of common gentility will reach the age of sixteen without altering her name as far as she can?), is what I would call my intimate friend and confidante. It is remarkable, however, that, when I was in Bath, the only occasion on which we have been separated for any length of time, she neither insisted on my writing by every post, nor exacted a promise of transmitting the character of every new acquaintance, nor a detail of every interesting conversation that Bath might produce. She is still at home, along with the little ones, George and Harriet, and I suppose that you would say that she is not yet out, although we have little room or use for such distinctions so tucked away as we are in the country.

As for the others, please forgive me if I avoid a detailed description. It would take far too long, and you would be extremely bored long before the end of it, for I fear that the gift of bringing characters to life on paper is not given to me. You will meet them all in the course of time, I hope, and then you will be far more capable of describing them to me than I ever could to you. Besides, I am longing to go on to a very different subject.

Thank you so much for the thought of bringing back a real Parisian dress for me. It is so good of you, and so like you. Tell me more, I beg you, of this magical creation. I so long to try it on. Even Mrs Allen has never had a gown actually made in Paris. But from what you say it sounds rather daring. Do you really think it will be suitable? I have neither your style, nor your courage to carry off anything very much out of the ordinary.

But I fear I must be serious, and make some learned and cultured remark about how I am longing to hear what you think of the collections in the Louvre. You did promise me such news did you not. It is the nearest I am ever likely to get to such riches of the art world, and I do value your opinion on them, as on many other things.

I fear I am but a giddy, uneducated country girl, and will never be good enough for Henry unless you stretch out your hand to the aid of

Your devoted friend,

Catherine.

Letter the Thirteenth :   **Lady Hapworth to Miss Morland**

Paris

25th December 1802

My very dear Catherine,

    I wish you all the success in the world with the Mozart. I am sure you will be able to manage something that will please Henry if you apply yourself, and I have never believed you to be shy of application.

    I wish you the very best of Christmas greetings, too, and shall think of you and your real English Christmas dinner when we sit down to dinner with His Excellency, and try how a French chef can mangle *le dindonneau* and *le plumpudding*. There is no escaping it, even if Charles were not attached to the embassy in some vague way that I have never quite fathomed. Every English person of any consequence in Paris will be there, and any absence is sure to be noticed. Christmas presents are such a bore that I will not waste your time with a description of mine from Charles, although when he found time to sneak to the Palais Royal to purchase it I have no idea. My memories of my mother grow more faded every day, such is human frailty, but one of them is of her once saying "one cannot have too many emeralds."

This bids fair to be rather a full day, and I am snatching a few moments to write to you as I do not know when I shall next have an opportunity.

I promised you a description of the famous gallery at the Louvre, or, rather the Musée Napoléon as it is now renamed. It is, of course, all crowded now with the finest pictures and sculptures of Italy, the plunder of a hundred battles and sieges, and one cannot help but be impressed. One also cannot help but wonder how long the paintings will stand the full sun that pours in through the many windows. I was always told that a gallery should be top lit, to preserve the colours, but no-one seems to have told Bonaparte that.

The sculptures are very fine, and I must confess that it is very convenient to be able to view the Laocöon and the Apollo Belvedere without the trouble of pursuing them to Florence or Rome. The weather is, of course, much warmer in Italy, and even more so in Greece, where their state of undress must have occasioned no more concern to the viewer than to the viewed.

Of the pictures, I thought Raphael's Transfiguration the finest, but it is so difficult to convey any useful description of any work of art of this stature that I do not propose even to try. Forgive me, my dear, but unless you see with your own eyes you can have no idea of the impression wrought upon one's sensibility by the sight of so many masterpieces, and almost all of then stolen. I am told that Bonaparte himself wrote back saying "We have stripped Italy of everything of artistic worth, with the exception of a few objects in Turin and Naples!"

The whole place, too, seems to be full of English people, either staring entranced or feverishly setting up their easels and making copies. I am sure I recognized Mr Opie, who took our likenesses when we were all children.

But excuse me, my dear, there seems to be some sort of commotion going on in the parlour, and I must see to it. Charles has apparently come back early from his call on the Ambassador and the servants are all in a panic.

Later.

I am now finishing this note in haste, as we are engaged for the rest of the day, and tomorrow we leave for Italy. Yes, for Italy! And in the middle of the winter!

The Alps, of course, will be impassable, and we should perforce be stranded somewhere up a mountain in a howling blizzard, vainly hoping for rescue by some mountaineer and his dog with its barrel of brandy round its neck, while our flickering fire slowly died and we awaited the inevitable end. Such an adventure as would no doubt suit you, my dear, especially if the mountaineer were handsome and could be persuaded to increase his speed. But I fear it is not to my taste at all, and I told Charles as much when he broke the news.

"The passes will all be blocked at this time of year." I said. "From all that we have heard, the crossing is difficult enough in spring and summer. In January it would be madness to try. Why may we not stay here in Paris until the warm weather?"

"There are reasons," he replied. "Paris is becoming less and less comfortable for foreigners of all descriptions, and particularly for the English.

Have you not remarked how the demeanour of the crowd has changed. Les Anglais are no longer quite so welcome as they were. Le Moniteur, too, is full of threatening articles sur le Perfide Albion."

"Newspapers!" I snorted, "They have copies to sell. They will make up anything they think the public will pay to read."

"Ours will. They order things differently in France, however. The newspapers here print exactly what the government tells them to print. If *Le Moniteur* says that the English are breaking the terms of the treaty of Amiens, and all good citizens must prepare to resist them, it is because that is what Bonaparte wishes the French people to believe. Bonaparte has no conception of a free press. The articles printed about him in England are a continual cause of complaints to the embassy. He simply cannot believe that they might reflect anyone's opinion but that of His Majesty's Government.

It is all designed to throw a screen over his own actions, of course, and to justify them. Our time here cannot last much longer."

"Tell me, then, O lord and master," I enquired, "are we, or are we not meant to be here on our honeymoon?"

"We are here on our honeymoon, and that is another reason why I must take care. The diplomatic papers I obtained by undertaking to carry highly confidential messages to Lord Whitworth will soon expire, and we must move on in any case. And the situation is not what it was when we arrived. The peace is failing. In the past twelve months, Bonaparte has broken one after another of the clauses in the treaty. He has sent an expedition to Santo Domingo; he has annexed Piedmont and Parma, he has had himself made President of the Cisalpine Republic, itself a creation of his own. He has refused to withdraw his troops from Holland. He has marched into Switzerland and refused to recognize our right to object. Diplomatic exchanges grow every day more bitter. It cannot be long now before there is open war. I want you out of here before that happens."

"But, surely, you do not expect us to be in danger if we remain here until the spring, as we planned?"

"The diplomatic passports were a mistake, it seems. They smoothed formalities on our way here, but as far as the French are concerned, anyone associated with the Embassy is a spy, and will be subject to who knows what restrictions should negotiations break down. That goes for you, too, my dear."

"But surely you do not mean that Bonaparte would have us taken up as spies, perhaps imprisoned?"

"Who knows what that man might do? I do not intend to take the risk."

"The passes will still be closed. If the situation is so bad, surely we would be better to make for the Channel Ports and home?"

"You said it yourself, my dear, we are on our honeymoon, and I do not propose to let any Frenchman – or Corsican – spoil it. I promised you the sights of Italy, and Italy you shall have. Bonaparte's writ does not run supreme there, yet, and we may still see the Leaning Tower, the Last Supper, the ruins of the Forum Romanum, perhaps even the fires of Vesuvius before we return home. Bonaparte may terrorise the land, but Britannia rules the waves, and there are ships from Genoa, from Leghorn, even from Naples that will take us safely home. There is little love for him in Rome, and less in the Two

Sicilies. Once across the Po we should be safe enough, for now."

"I have your knowledge of neither politics, nor, it seems, geography, my dear, but all that can make no difference to the weather. How are we to attain this Transpadane refuge of yours? There is no way through the snows of the Alps."

"I know a trick worth two of that, my love. I may not be a spy, but I do have my sources of information, and I think I may safely promise to have you sight the Hesperian shores before three weeks are out, and with, I sincerely hope, no symptoms of the fell frost-bite. Leave it all to me, but be ready betimes in the morning."

"But it's Christmas!" was all I could think of to say, and I fear I gaped, rather.

"So it is. And if it was not for this wretched dinner of His Excellency's we should have left yesterday. Now I must go dress for the confounded nuisance. The coach is ordered for ten o' clock tomorrow. Be ready."

Dear Charles! He can be so deliciously masterful when he wishes.

So you see, my pet, I must conclude. I have no idea when my next letter shall be, nor where it may be from, nor where to ask you to send any reply to this.

I seem to have fallen into one of the adventures which you are so fond of reading about, and can only hope and pray that you will soon hear from

Your Gothickally- enmired friend,

Eleanor.

Letter the Fourteenth :   Lady Hapworth to Miss Morland

Toulouse

2nd January 1803

My dear Catherine,

The very best of New Year greetings to you, from a city which I believe would charm you quite to a degree. Here you could indulge in your Gothick imaginings quite to excess. The twisty mediaeval streets, the old buildings, the memories of the Albigensians, all add up to an atmosphere I believe you would call romantic.

I, however, am pleased to call it civilized, although, certainly, as for the view of the cathedral from where I am sitting, "even when lighted up by the setting sun, the gothic greatness of its features, and its mouldering walls of dark grey stone, render it a gloomy and sublime object." See, I can quote *Udolpho* with the best of them, when I wish to. At the moment I do not particularly wish to, however. After seven days on the road from Paris (and French roads, at that), I am disposed to look very favourably on anywhere that can provide soft beds and hot baths.

How we got here is a tale in itself, and a tribute to the admirable ingenuity and perseverance of my dear husband, who never ceases to amaze me. From all I have been told, it usually takes months to traverse France, certainly in the lumbering diligences one sees everywhere, crawling along at little more than walking pace, and that is in the summer, when the roads are at their best. We, however, had a carriage to ourselves, somewhat like a post-chaise, but differing in various Gallic details, the chief of which was the number of horses. I was quite intrigued when I looked out of the window and saw there were but three, and that our bags were already being piled into its boot. Charles, too, had never before seen such a sight, and hurried down to reason with the driver.

From my vantage point I caught only the odd word or phrase in reply to my beloved's demand for the fourth horse, of which "Ça ne se fait jamais" seemed to be the most often repeated, until there was the clink of money changing hands and the fellow dashed off to reappear less than five minutes later with not one, but two extra horses, and it was behind this unlikely team that we sped off, five in hand, into a frosty, but mercifully snow-free morning.

"The mumping villain," said Charles after we had adjusted the rugs and furs to the best effect (I will not say to our satisfaction, for there is no such thing as satisfaction when striving to stop the draughts in a French carriage). "All he was waiting for was the sight of English gold. He had those horses ready stationed round the corner, or he could not have been back with them so quickly. Still, I have promised him more if he gets us to our destination within a week, and to do that, he will have to earn it."

Naturally, I enquired how we could possibly get to the Alps, let alone across them, in a week, but he only smiled and said "Wait and see, my love."

How I do hate it when he goes all mysterious, *Udolpho* or no.

To give Gaston his due, he did earn his money, urging our horses on through all weathers as long as the light lasted, changing them every hour so as to keep up the pace, and depositing us in the best lodging to be had at the end of each day.

But, oh, my dear, these French country inns! The merest barns, barely furnished, where the bulk of their clients sleep on straw in the common room when the tables have been cleared away. The to-do we had to obtain some semblance of privacy in some of these places you would scarcely credit. Fortunately, good English gold is as efficacious as ever, though I begin to wonder how much further we can get before Charles must cash another letter of credit. Nothing, however, not even *"l'or maudit du Perfide Albion"* is efficacious against the denizens of French mattresses, and hot water, and plenty of it, is now my first care.

The French, conversely, care nothing for the squalor in which they must pass the night. For them it is the quality of the food that matters, and it must be admitted that it has all been very tasty, my dear, although at times one scarcely knows what it is that one is eating, and is perhaps better off for that. I have not positively sighted any frogs or snails yet, but there have certainly been some very mysterious dishes served up to us.

At least we may be sure that we have not been singled out for special treatment, since all must gather round the same board and take the same table d'hôte, usually from the one big bowl. There have been some very strange messes indeed, but there has also been some splendid *poule au pot,* and *civet de lièvre.*

    All this inconvenience was in the name of confidentiality, too. I should have said secrecy, were the word not too ridiculous. There were several sizeable cities, with reputable hotels, where we could have passed our nights had Charles not been so insistent on not being noticed. I was sure we should have stopped at Orleans, and then at Limoges, but neither was to be.

    What a relief it is, at last, to find oneself in a city again, with what passes for modern conveniences in this part of France, with the prospect of a whole day, at least, without being shut up in a bumping, bouncing carriage, with the draught chilling one to the bone no matter how many layers one is swathed in, and the snow seeping round the edges of the windows and doors. Why ever does one go a-travelling?

    There is no trace of snow here in Toulouse, however, and already the weather grows noticeably warmer- or perhaps it is only less cold than the winter roads, but even so, it is very welcome. It is marvellous the effect of an uninterrupted night's sleep in a real feather bed, can have, especially when combined with a hot bath and strong French coffee. Croissants are but a poor substitute for a real breakfast, of which the French have no notion, but they do very well for starters.

I have the happy prospect of a day of rest today, but Charles says we must set off again tomorrow. I intend to make the most of that rest from travelling (I feel I know, now, why so many inns are called "The Traveller's Rest"), so I beg you to excuse me further description of the city and its curiosities, which I fear are not curious enough to tempt me away from my comfort.

Charles is still being mysterious about our onward journey, so I cannot say when I shall next be able to write to you. Nor can I give you any specific direction to which you may address your next - which I am longing to receive, I may add. All I know is that we are bound for Genoa at the moment, and a line to Poste Restante, Genova would greatly oblige

Your peripatetic friend,

Eleanor.

Letter the Fifteenth : Lady Hapworth to Miss Morland

Canal du Midi

4th January 1803

Dear Catherine,

I am writing this as I loll upon a sofa in perfect comfort, and survey the French countryside outside. Yet I am not stealing another day off from our travels, nor have I persuaded Charles to postpone or curtail them, for the French countryside I am surveying is moving rather rapidly past my window, and I am getting nearer our destination with every word I write.

"How can this be?" you may ask.

Well, I will confess to have misled you in my last paragraph. The countryside is not moving, but I am. The apparent motion past my window is an illusion caused by the perfect steadiness of the platform on which I am myself moving. The window through which I am looking is that of our cabin on the barge *"Citoyenne Julie"*, on the *Canal du Midi*, or the *Canal de las Doas Mars*, as the crew call it, which connects the river Garonne at Toulouse with the Étang de Thau on the Mediterranean, enabling boats of some considerable size to sail from sea to sea with perfect ease.

Our boat is certainly of not inconsiderable size, some hundred feet long, but quite narrow withal, enabling it to maintain a speed which allows it to pass from one end of the canal to the other in but four days, with horses changed every eight or nine miles.

Most of the traffic on the water consists of cargo barges, carrying the wheat, wine and brandy of the Languedoc to Toulouse, Bordeaux and Marseilles and bringing back rice, starch, dried fish, spices, dyes and the famous *savon de Marseille*. See what an expert I am become on the economy of southern France! I love Charles dearly, but he can be given to lecturing at times.

But *our* boat spurns all these menial tasks. It is a *Malle de Poste*, and carries only mail and passengers. It stops only at the principal mail stations, and takes pride in keeping its time. In France, everything stops pour le déjeuner, but we do not. It is served to us on tables in the salon which occupies most of the front half of the boat. The common passengers must sleep there, too, but those of the first class have their own cabins, fitted out quite like the Dover Packet, or rather better, and much more comfortable, as the water through which we move is perfectly still, and does not give rise to the feelings of discomfort that so often plague travellers by sea. There are bunks and chairs and tables that let down from the sides, and even the little necessities are perfectly catered for in a tiny closet that empties into the canal. I slept perfectly last night. Compared to last week's coach travel, this is paradise.

Even paradise has it longeurs, however, and I have been amusing myself, when the sight of the passing countryside palls, with going over your old letters, beginning with the very first, in which you mention, among other things, that you have never met my Charles.

But my dear, you have! That is to say, you have not been mutually introduced, but you have been in each other's presence, if only for a very short while. Do you remember one morning when we were walking in the hanger, and Henry drew you on while

I remained in converse with a young man who had come upon us as we walked? That man was my Charles. I apologise for not introducing you at the time, but there were reasons for discretion, as I hope I shall soon make clear. The *tête à tête* we had on that occasion concerned his leaving our neighbourhood, and his home, to take up a post under government with his cousin, the then viscount. The nature of that post was never made clear at the time, and still has not been, although it appears to be of a vaguely diplomatic nature. He was *persona non grata* at Northanger Abbey then, but could not go without taking his leave of me. It was typical of Henry's tact and consideration that he should contrive to leave us alone together for a short while.

Dear Charles! I dare say you would not rate him very highly as a hero, my dear. He has rescued me from no bandits, fought no dragons for me, broken no lances in jousts while wearing my favour, but he is my hero nonetheless.

He did once fight an entire host on my behalf, battling his way through truly formidable foes to bring me an ice, the first of all to be consumed at that party. We were seven years old at the time, and I have been in love with him ever since. He is, perhaps, not so brave as Frederick, nor so witty as Henry, nor so generally delightful and obliging as you, my dear, but to me he is the sweetest, kindest, best man on the planet. As an example of his kindness I need only cite the morning we set off on our present journey. We had had, you may recollect, something of a disagreement the previous evening, when I was not best pleased with his design of leaving Paris immediately. I was woken the following morning by the sound of music in the street outside, and on going to the window beheld a band of street musicians playing a tune which I recognized. At their head was Charles, playing manfully on the guitar and singing an aria which I recognized as from Tolomeo by Mr Handel. This is not to say that I am an expert on musicians of the last age, but this particular one was a favourite of my mother's. His light tenor voice as he sang the words –

> *"Though I am nothing to her,*
>
> *Though she may never think of me,*
>
> *Though I may never woo her,*
>
> *I love her till I die."*

took me right back to my childhood, indeed to

that same party where we plundered the ices as my mother sang that very song. How could I continue unkind with such a man?

We made up our minds very early to marry (I think it was the second ice that secured it), and why should we not? We had been friends from childhood, played together since we were both in long frocks, grown up together. We knew each other's minds and hearts far better than any other ever could. But we may not please only ourselves in this world.

Henry was delighted when we told him. He knew Charles's worth and appreciated it. Frederick, on the other hand, was scornful but insouciant. The obstacle was my father. You have suffered from his inconsistency yourself, my dear, and will have some notion of how I felt when my love turned overnight from an honoured guest to a pariah never to show his face within our home again. The cause of this transformation was, of course, his request to my father for my hand in marriage.

It had never occurred to either of us that he would refuse. Charles had always been welcome at Northanger Abbey. The Covenhams were our nearest neighbours. They were a family old and renowned in the county, and had once held wide estates. Indeed, in King Henry's day, the Covenhams of Northanger Monachorum were of quite as much consequence as the Tilneys of Northanger Abbas. They chose the wrong side in the Civil War, however, and on King Charles's restoration, were punished by losing half of their land to their loyal neighbours, the Tilneys. Since then, mismanagement and gambling debts had further reduced the estate, so that by now it was barely able to support a gentleman and his family.

No "five hundred a year country squire who ekes out a living as a glorified errand boy for his relatives" should have General Tilney's daughter, it transpired. She was reserved for worthier things, and was to be the means by which the Tilney family would be ennobled, the lucky peer to be selected at the General's leisure. For having the effrontery to suggest a different course, young Mr Covenham was bundled out of the house in such haste that he left behind the pile of documents you afterwards found. Yes, my Catherine, those were his washbills you found, it was his room you occupied, and his bed you slept in. I leave it to you, my dear, whether you reveal to your family that you have slept in the same bed as a viscount. I do not know them well enough to guess how they would take such news.

That was my sad state when you came to Northanger. The trip to Bath had been settled upon as a treat, to "bring me out of my moping", and, to a degree, it worked, especially after our friendship began to progress. I think I hid it well enough, did I not, but, looking back, I see that my heart was breaking, and it was only by busying myself with you that I was able to bear it. The love of my life had been banished the house, and was about to leave the country, never, perhaps, to return. I had, as far as I could see, no hope of avoiding being traded like a leg of mutton to some fat Duke or Earl, so that my father could have the satisfaction of referring to "His daughter, Lady So-and-so". Your sweet innocence, yes, and the love that I could see growing between you and Henry, were my comforts in those days.

The unlikely series of chances by which Charles became heir to his distant cousin Hapworth would scarce be credited in one of your Gothick novels, with their shipwrecks, their lightning strikes, their garrottings in the back streets of Naples, and the sheer number of apoplexies and downright declines involved.

But behold me, at the end of it all, a viscountess, married to the man I love, and - I have just realized - perhaps on the way to those same back streets myself, or others just as disreputable. Lightning, they say never strikes twice, and I promise you I shall take very great care to avoid the garrotte, but I fear there will always be scope for a shipwreck until I am safely on English soil again. I am perfectly familiar with the English terror and distaste for foreign parts, where only the worst can be expected to happen, and I assure you that the most tangible danger I have so far encountered has been that of catching a cold while wearing the latest Paris fashion in the winter.

I do admit, however, that the sheer, continual, unrelenting foreignness of everything on all sides does get me down from time to time, especially these last few days when the only English voice I have heard has been that of Charles. It is a perfectly delightful voice, but even delight, when it is unvarying, can be wearing.

But we are pulling in to a post station, and I must take care to send this off while there is the opportunity.

I will write to you again from Genoa, if not before. Write to me there, if you would be so kind, and ease the heart of

Your loving friend,

Eleanor

Letter the Sixteenth : Miss Morland to Lady Hapworth, in Genoa

Northanger Abbey

6th January 1803

My very dear Eleanor,

Yes, you may well stretch your eyes at the superscription, but it is true.

We have been here nearly a fortnight now, and must soon go home. Henry turned up at Fullerton on the day after Christmas, not in his own gig as usual, but in the full grandeur of the General's barouche-landau, bearing an invitation from his father for the whole family to welcome in the new year with him.

"And not before time," said Henry. "It is well past time that all misunderstandings between my father and my future wife were cleared away and buried, and he is seeing sense at last. He languishes all alone at Northanger with my sister gone and Frederick away with his regiment, and he knows that

I shall certainly not spend the holiday with him unless you are there, too, my darling."

Sally and the boys were wild to go, there and then, but my father said that he could not in conscience leave his parishioners at this time, and then, of course, my mother refused to leave him, nor to let the boys go with only their sad, scatter-brained sisters to look after them, so in the end it was only Sally and I who returned with Henry, rattling around in the vast conveyance.

I stipulated, however, that any letters received for me at Fullerton in my absence were immediately to be transmitted to Northanger, and the General has been so kind as to send a man over for me every day especially.

Sally was all agog to see the scene of my great adventure, which has lost nothing in the telling by the family fireside. Besides, the popular novels she spends the chief of her time reading, although they may be work in which the greatest powers of the mind are displayed, in which the most thorough knowledge of human nature, the happiest delineation of its varieties, the liveliest effusions of wit and humour, are conveyed to the world in the best-chosen language - as I believe to have heard somebody else say once upon a time - have given her a very exalted idea of any place whose name includes the word "Abbey". I feared she might be disappointed when we reached the end of our journey, but she seems happy enough. She is but seventeen after all.

But in the end it was all a terrible sell, for the General has other guests, whom I fear he has invited especially to revive his old design. They are the dowager Lady Lumpton and her daughter, the Honourable Lavinia, the latter of whom he seems determined to throw in Henry's way as much as possible.

At dinner on the first night, and ever since, he has taken care that the Honourable Lavinia should sit next to Henry, and both he and the dowager have been at pains to detach us from each other at other times. Nor did he introduce me as Henry's fiancée, but merely as a "dear friend of my daughter, Viscountess Hapworth".

I fear that in the continued absence of the lady viscountess, and her moderating influence, his old designs may have revived.

But pray take no heed of my missish jealousies.

I am sure that Henry is proof against all blandishments, and am more concerned at how terrible it must have been for you, to be rushed out of Paris in such a headlong fashion! Can it be true that after all the years we suffered from the privations of war, we are about to embark upon a new one after scarcely more than a year of peace? And yet the newspapers are ominous enough, to be sure, even here in our rural seclusion.

Bonaparte's treatment of the poor Swiss opened our eyes here more than anything else, I think. That is what Henry says, at any rate, and he encourages me to take an interest in what is going on in the world. Otherwise I should hardly dare to venture an opinion, least of all to you, who are so wise, and are actually in the middle of it all.

I do hope there will not be another war, especially as it will necessarily involve so many places you must pass through. Do you really think you will be safe in Italy? Did not Bonaparte transform Genoa into the Ligurian Republic or some such? And has he not just occupied Piedmont, which is quite next door on our old atlas? I wish I understood these things better. I must ask Henry. He always explains everything so clearly.

I assure you, it is *my* heart that will be eased by hearing from you. Until I do, I shall be on tenterhooks.

Your mode of travel from Toulouse sounds just the thing that might tempt me to go abroad, were such a thing possible. No bumping over dusty roads, no hurried snacks at halts, sleeping in a proper bed, and you wake up in a new place every morning. And such speed! Henry says that to get on as you do, you must be going at an average rate of some ten miles an hour, day and night. It is scarcely to be wondered at that you should make such progress.

If only it were bringing you closer, rather than taking you further away from us all, how much happier such velocity would make

Your loving friend

Catherine.

P.S.

News is just come in of Mr Sheridan's speech in parliament against Bonaparte. In case it has not reached you yet, I will repeat the quotations from Mr

Allen's newspaper –

"I see in the physical situation and composition of the power of Bonaparte a physical necessity for him to go on in this barter with his subjects and to promise to make them masters of the world if they will consent to be his slaves."

He goes on to say that he can only do so by conquering England, and this "is the first vision that breaks upon him through the gleam of morning: that is his last prayer at night, to whatever deity he may address it, whether to Jupiter or to Mahomet, to the Goddess of Battles or to the Goddess of Reason."

These are strong words, are they not, and Bonaparte is reported to be much angered by them. The general feeling here is that the peace cannot last much longer.

I am only an ignorant girl, and may be taking alarm unnecessarily, but do you not think it would be wiser to come home? Henry has authorized me to ask you, or I should not dare.

You may have reason for confidence in your continued safety while within reach of the Tyrant, but if so, we should all be glad to hear of it.

Letter the Seventeenth :   Lady Hapworth to Miss Morland

Béziers

5th January 1803

Dear Catherine,

I could not resist writing to you from here, partly because I never know where my next post office will be, but also because I am sure you would be delighted with the scene from where I am sitting.

We have abandoned the barge for a few hours while it negotiates the Écluse de Fonserannes, a "ladder", or series of eight locks with nine lock gates, which barges must negotiate to circumnavigate this charming old city. These locks are the greatest impediment to travel on the canals, and can easily take up half of the day, if the traffic is heavy. The traffic *is* rather heavy at the moment, but practically all of it is northbound. Charles tells me it is munitions and foodstuffs going to Bonaparte's armies, but how he can possibly know as much I have no idea. He has persuaded himself that another war is imminent, and sees signs of it everywhere.

Why there should be so many of these locks I cannot fathom. One never meets with this sort of thing on a river, after all. The barge must take up station behind a great gate, stretched right across the canal at a narrow point, while another gate is closed behind it. If one peeps over the first gate, one may observe that the water beyond it is at a much lower level. When both gates are closed, by some contrivance the water beneath the boat begins to sink, until at last the front gate is opened, and one passes out onto the lower stretch. Charles spent a great deal of time explaining the workings, and the purpose of the mechanism, but I fear I did not attend, being too busy enjoying the sunshine and the balmy breezes to pay him much heed. I gather it is something to do with stopping all the water in the canal pouring out into the sea, but more than that I could not say.

But, Catherine, it is warm down here in the South, like an English spring day. We are sitting on a terrace at the back of the cathedral, with a view down to the river, and I cannot help thinking of the dreadful

Albigensian Crusade, and of the pope's reply to Simon de Montfort when he asked what he should do with his prisoners, and how he could tell Cathars from Catholics.

"Burn them all," was the pontiff's reply. "God will know his own."

What a terrible contrast the scene then must have made with the peaceful landscape stretched before my eyes now! I positively decline to exercise my imagination upon the smoke from a thousand fires, the screams of the dying, and the terrible desolation that day must have brought. And now, all is peaceful, beautiful, yes, serene. What a strange world we live in!

Forgive me, my dear, I have been cooped up in a boat for too long, and it brings on strange fancies. I believe the mariners call it "shake crazy" or some such term.

It is a pleasure in itself to be able to walk about on dry land, and see houses and shops again.

But our voyage will soon be over, for tomorrow we reach Cette, where we must transship for the next leg of our journey, which will involve the open sea.

Memories of the crossing from Dover to Calais crowd in, just when I had hoped them forgotten forever. I fear I am no born sailor, and cannot convince myself not to believe that I shall disgrace myself soon enough. The phrase *"mal de mer"* is French, after all, is it not?

At least here in the south, France seems less bellicose, more normal. There are the odd *mutilés de guerre* on the street corners, but, so far at least, we have seen none of the crowds of soldiers that throng the streets of Paris. I cannot say that the people are well-disposed towards us, however, and I begin to think that perhaps it is as well that we shall soon be leaving them.

In fact, I long for Genoa, in the hope and expectation that there I will find waiting a letter from you, to be seized upon, opened and greedily read by

Your impatient friend

Eleanor

Letter the Eighteenth : Lady Hapworth to Miss Morland

Marseilles

9th January 1803

My very dear Catherine,

The day after my last, we disembarked the *Bonne Citoyenne* at Cette, a queer sort of place seemingly built especially as the terminus of the canal. It is totally maritime in its nature, and utterly undistinguished in its buildings apart from the ever-present hand of M. Vauban in the fortifications that surround it, like so many French towns. One of the passengers told me that it is known as the "Venice of Languedoc" because of its numerous canals, but I saw no evidence of this. Perhaps a longer stay would have convinced me of its charms, but I doubt it.

We stayed there only as long as it took to disembark our barge and transfer to the coasting vessel which brought us to Marseilles. The *Droits de l'Homme* was a mere tub, completely unworthy the grandiose name, half the size of the barge which brought us down from Toulouse, with accommodations in proportion. Her single mast bore a curiously shaped sail of an ochreish colour, which Charles tells me is called a tartan, although it bears no resemblance to the chequered cloth of the barbarous Highlander. We were the only passengers, and the crew spoke some sort of incomprehensible southern gabble, so I have no encounters or anecdotes to relate of the voyage.

The coast east of Cette, which was visible throughout the first day, is very flat and undistinguished, and I do not propose to notice it. What is very worthy of notice, however, is the Mediterranean sea itself. The first thing that strikes you about it is the colour, a vibrant, brilliant blue, as unlike our muddy, grey-green English seas as a peacock to a sparrow. One could look at it all day, which, I suppose, was just as well, since no other objects of view appeared. Then there is the extreme clarity of the water, such as one could not imagine if one had never seen it. The sea bed itself is displayed to the eye, and all the fishes and other creatures swimming about in it. Charles pointed one out which he said was a shark, and cautioned me not to fall overboard lest I be eaten before I could be rescued.

How he does love to make my flesh creep!

I mentioned that there was nothing to look at but the sea, but that is not strictly true, since it was dotted all over with sails of all colours, mostly quite as curiously shaped as ours. The traffic along this coast seems very busy, and most of it going from Italy to France. The master of our vessel jabbered something to us which I took to mean that they were bringing supplies to be ferried up the canal and transported onward to supply Bonaparte's armies. He was, however, perfectly polite, assuring us that "nos amis, les Anglais" need have no fear of the First Consul's entirely peaceful intentions as he gave orders for folding chairs to be erected for us on the quarterdeck.

From these chairs we surveyed the day with as little discomfort as might be expected while travelling, for to retire to our stuffy cupboard of a cabin while this warm breeze blew could not be contemplated. In the middle of the afternoon we were rewarded by the sight of small fish leaping from the sea, seemingly gliding along on their fins for some distance before falling back to the element. The crew seemed perfectly unconcerned by this, and distinctly amused by my exclamations of astonished delight.

Charles, as a rule, does not indulge in either astonishment or delight, or at least not in public, but even he could not entirely disguise his interest.

Yes, my dear, I have seen the famous flying fish! Well may you envy me, though I do gloat! But there was more to come, for it appears that these remarkable fish only take to the air when attempting to escape their predators, and in this case those predators were a group of dolphins, who soon, however, lost interest in their prey and began gambolling around our ship, leaping out of the water in perfect arcs, diving underneath us from one side to the other, and generally making sport. We have all heard tales of the dolphin's friendliness to man, of its rescuing shipwrecked sailors and the like, but, until now, I had thought of them as tales only, no more veracious than Jack and the Beanstalk, or Aladdin and his Lamp. But now I have seen them with my own eyes, and can no longer doubt. What other wonders and new sensations might our travels yet disclose?

To emphasise that we are in historic waters, just as the sun was setting, Charles pointed out a speck in the far distance which he said was Aigues Mortes, whence Saint Louis set out on his crusades, but it might as well have been Bristol or Brighton or Birmingham for all that I could make out. Thereafter there was nothing to be seen save the reflection of the moon upon the water, and we retired to our cupboard for the night.

The morning brought Marseilles into sight. It also brought an end to the steady wind which had blown the day before from the west and sped us so expeditiously on our way. The frustration of lying motionless for half the day with the end of one's journey in sight must be a common incident of sea travel, but the sensation, though certainly new, was far from congenial. The mariners, presumably long-inured to this sort of thing, amused themselves by completing tasks which had apparently been put off for just such an opportunity, but we were left to yawn and make faces at each other to pass the time. I could not even write to you, as my desk had been packed away into the hold when we embarked. I did think to ask Charles of our future plans, and why he was really in such a hurry to reach Italy, but the only answer I received was "Not now. Not here. Later."

This was sufficiently unlike his usual style as to silence me quite effectively, and to make me begin to feel as worried as he had been looking for the past week.

But, however, in the middle of the afternoon, a light wind arose from the south, and strengthened gradually as it bore us into harbour. The lights were going on all along the quayside as we passed between the forts of St. John and St. Nicholas which guard the entrance.

The impression I got was of a port almost entirely naval. Three frigates and an eighty-four gun ship were moored alongside the forts, two to each side, but the rest of the quayside showed only small, coastal vessels like our own. Charles tells me that the presence of such a squadron here is unusual, however, as the bulk of the French fleet usually lies at Toulon, which is, as it were, their Portsmouth.

The forts are impressive, but the rest of the town much less so, although the Vieille Charité, an imposing great structure in the middle of a maze of alleyways, must be the most grandiose set of almshouses ever built, with its colonnades and domes and fussily decorated baroque chapel.

It pleased Charles to think that we now stood on antique soil, in a harbour that had been used not merely by the Romans, but by the Greeks before them. The conceit had not occurred to me, but he took such delight in it that, of course, it pleased me too.

We stay here only one night, for tomorrow we take ship for Genoa. This will be the first time we venture out of sight of land, and already I am feeling queasy.

I know that by the time this reaches you it will be too late, but, even so, pray wish calm seas and a prosperous voyage for

Your shamefully timorous sister

Eleanor

Letter the Nineteenth : Lady Hapworth to Miss Morland

Genoa

15th January 1803

My dear Catherine,

What a joy it was to open your letter! I feel that I have been writing letters and receiving none for so long that I am become an outcast. The feeling is not helped by my inability to understand all but the odd word of the myriads I hear pronounced around me here.

After speaking French for so long I rather pride myself on my fluency, but here I might as well be mute. My Italian, of course, is merely what may be expected of any English lady who has been decently educated, that is to say, only knowledge enough of the language to translate at sight a few inverted, transposed, curtailed Italian lines, *on paper*, into clear, comprehensible, elegant English. With this I was content until I came here, but those few lines, however transposed or curtailed, must at least be in Tuscan, to which the barbarous argot spoken in the streets of Genoa bears, as far as I can tell, very little resemblance, if any at all. That, combined with the

Italian sense of urgency and the French love of form-filling which has infected their subjects, meant that it took half the day before I could get your letter out of the hands of the post office clerks, and then only when silver had changed hands.

But however, all that looks like to change, thanks to a very peculiar incident which I will relate to you shortly.

First, however, let me get the voyage from Marseilles out of the way. The delights of the trip from Cette had almost converted me to sea travel, at least in warmer climes, but I fear my nature is not so easily changed. The choppy seas and contumacious winds we encountered have quite destroyed the trust I had built up in the Mediterranean as a medium of transit, and I must make shift to conceal my contentment when Charles chafes at being held up here for who knows how many days, all on account of the wind. We are penned in by the dread Sirocco, a warm wind that blows constantly from the south, and bestows upon the city a perfect mildness of climate in the winter for as long as it continues. It will not do for a voyage further along the Italian coast, however. For that we need the fell Tramontana, the icy wind from the north that turns the narrow streets into perfect funnels for the for the icy draft. You may easily see that this is a maritime city by the winds all having their own names here, and their own epithets, too, and none of those epithets is a grateful one, for, to the mariner, each wind has its own peculiar terrors.

Genoa is a strange city to our northern eyes, tightly pressed onto the seashore by the mountains that so nearly surround it. The town within the walls is such a warren of narrow streets as I have never seen, with the most extreme squalor and gorgeous splendour set side by side, and entire streets of palaces seemingly marooned in the midst of teeming rookeries. The Via del Duomo is broad enough, but every other street but one looks like something from an Italian opera seria of the most depressing kind, while the cathedral itself, with its black and white stripes, looks exceeding odd to one used to our Gothick church buildings.

As for the people themselves who swarm within these narrow alleys, their constant exclaiming and gesticulating makes me wonder how I could ever have found Paris noisy. Compared to an Italian market place, the busiest Parisian street is but a rest cure.

But, to return to the incident of which I promised you a relation, we were walking along the Strada Nuova - a street even broader than the Via del Duomo, and lined, it seems, entirely with palaces - having finally gained possession of your letter, and some others for Charles, when we were greeted by a young man of vaguely familiar appearance.

"Well, bless my soul!" he exclaimed, with an extravagant bow. "Miss Tilney, is it not? John Thorpe, ma'am, at your service. We met at Bath, last year, if you remember. I was there with my sister, and we all had such fun together, with you, and your brother, and Miss Morland."

That was not exactly how I should have phrased it, nor, I think, would you, my dear, but, of course, I knew him once he said his name.

He was looking thinner than he did in Bath, his hair has grown and he has acquired a tan that would pass for an Italian, which explains how I did not know him at first.

He also looks even shabbier than he did in Bath, where he always did appear slightly seedy.

Had I seen him first, I should have avoided the

meeting, but as it was, I felt obliged to introduce him to "My husband, Viscount Hapworth."

The bow he made Charles was even more exaggerated than the one he had accorded to me on first accosting us, and I lost count of the number of "my lords" and "your lordships" he managed to introduce to his request for the exquisite honour and pleasure of making his sister known to such august company, and the earnest desire he had of being useful in any way at all to us.

"I am always glad to meet old friends of Lady Hapworth's," was Charles's reply to this exhibition, "but, pray, tell me, Mr Thorpe, what brings you to Genoa? Are you and your sister, like us, taking the opportunity provided by the present peace to make the Grand Tour?"

Mr Thorpe looked shiftier than ever, though perhaps I do him an injustice and the way he glanced furtively about him before replying is just a mannerism of his.

"Not exactly, my Lord, although of course we should greatly love to be in a position to do so," he said. "My Lady Viscountess is acquainted with my circumstances, so I will not attempt to make any such claim, however. The unvarnished truth is that certain circumstances, certain regrettable misunderstandings about a few trifling debts, made England an uncomfortable place for us, for the time being. The peace falling in so opportunely, and France being by repute so much more reasonable a place to live in, we thought we should try our fortunes there."

"I see. And how did those fortunes fare, Mr Thorpe? Tolerably well, I hope?"

"France, my Lord, was dashed disappointing. Tradesmen there are as perfectly unreasonable as they are in England. We found it necessary to move on from Paris to Orleans, and from Orleans to Lyon, and so down to Toulon and on to Mentone. We have been in Genoa for a month now, and I fear we must soon move on again."

At this, Charles merely bowed, and we were about to resume our course when I found my arm positively clutched by Mr Thorpe.

"Miss Tilney," he cried, in a voice quite unlike his usual sneering tone, "that is to say, my Lady, I beg of you to allow me and my sister to be of use to you. I know all the ins and out of this deuced city, and I can make myself understood in the local lingo.

And you won't find a better judge of horseflesh anywhere. The fact is we are hopelessly pushed for the readies, and almost desperate for an expedient. We do not ask for charity. Any sort of work you could offer we should be very glad to undertake. You know me, you know my sister, and you know just how much we may be relied upon. Please put in a good word for us with your noble husband, I beg you."

"Let there be no misunderstanding here, Mr Thorpe," I replied. "I believe I do know exactly how much you may be relied upon. Am I to understand that you are asking for employment as some variety of upper groom, or servant?"

"Well, not quite that, you know. What I had in mind was more like a sort of confidential agent, or steward, someone who could oil the wheels for you in this place, get things done for you, that sort of thing."

"My husband does not require a bear-leader, Mr Thorpe, nor am I in want of a companion." I replied, and would have moved on there and then, had Charles not interrupted.

"Come, come, my dear," he said. "We must not

throw off your dear old friend in such a cavalier fashion. We must consider of his proposal, and talk it over among ourselves."

"Mr Thorpe," he continued, turning to our interlocutor, "We are but newly landed from the Marseilles packet, where our bags still lie. The post office here was our first port of call, and we have not yet secured lodgings. No – do not offer to find suitable accommodation for me. I have friends I intend to call upon for that purpose. But I cannot, as yet give you a direction where you might find me. Where may we seek you, over the course of the next few days?"

Mr Thorpe appeared at first strangely reluctant to disclose his direction, but, after what was evidently some little consideration, he eventually replied -

"My sister and I lodge on the Via Maddalena, at the Angelo d'Oro."

A little further hesitation followed, before he continued, rather diffidently, I thought,

"It is but a stone's throw from here. Would you not step round and permit me to introduce her? She would be delighted to welcome you, I am sure."

"Then she is a most unusual lady. All those *I* know would be horrified at the very idea of such an impromptu visit, being forced to receive unexpected guests with the room all at sixes and sevens about them. We shall find you at the Golden Angel, then. Today is Saturday. Shall we say Monday, in the forenoon? Until then, good day, Mr Thorpe."

This time we did make good our escape, and I had to wait until we had rounded the corner on the way back to the harbour before I could ask what on earth he meant by this promise, and who were these friends to which he had alluded just now but never mentioned before.

"I have no doubt that at least one friend of that sort will be forthcoming when we have called upon the consul" he replied. " Meanwhile I did not wish to be beholden to your Mr Thorpe in any way, nor to put you in a position of having to offend him by refusing any lodgings he might endorse. I have no doubt that such apartments would be entirely unsuitable, and their only recommendation would be the commission they paid upon our introduction. I may, perhaps, misjudge your friend, but I think not."

"He is not *my* Mr Thorpe, nor is he my friend.

He is not exactly my enemy, I own, but neither he nor his sister are persons with whom I would wish to prolong my acquaintance, still less, initiate yours, my dear."

"Well, then, my darling, let us sit at this convenient terrace, and take a cup of the excellent Genoese coffee, while I unfold my purpose to you."

And he began pointedly to talk of the weather, until the waiter had left us with the "caffe con cannoli" that he had ordered. He can be so infuriating at times!

"I recommend to you most heartily," he continued, "these pastry tubes of which the Genoese are so fond. They fill them with a kind of cream cheese flavoured with, I believe, honey, vanilla and rosewater, and they are deservedly famous."

He suited his actions to his words, looking about us all the while, and uttering exclamations of inarticulate delight.

I was on the point of throwing my own pastry at him when he grinned, and held up a hand.

"Peace, my love," he said. "I was but playing my part as tourist, and making as sure as I can that we are not presently being observed. Tell me, my dear, are you aware that your Suzette is in the pay of M. de Talleyrand, and reports our every movement to her master?"

"Of course not. How can you ask such a question? She has always been perfectly faithful and reliable."

"Perhaps I wrong her. But I am pretty well convinced that my Pierrot reports to M. Fouché. I set a trap for him while we were in Béziers, leaving letters for him to find in which I mentioned certain plans – plans, I may assure you, which bore not the slightest resemblance to reality – which I now find to have been forwarded to Paris. The clerk at the post office was most obliging while you were taking the air, and when I mentioned that I believed my servant had left a letter there earlier today and described both him and a golden guinea, he made no difficulty in finding the item and allowing me to inspect it. Its contents were, apparently, gibberish, but its addressee was known to me, although not, apparently, to the clerk. He was most sympathetic when I explained that my servant, poor man, had this mania about certain officials of the French government, and had constantly to be prevented from bombarding them with nonsensical correspondence, and agreed with me entirely that we must make every effort to prevent the time of such an important person being wasted by the effusions of an otherwise harmless lunatic. I have the letter with me now, and shall try my hand at breaking the code when we are settled in. But that explains all the odd little things I have been noticing ever since we left Paris, and why Master Pierrot was in such a terrible hurry to leave the ship this morning, before we were even out of our beds, as the shipmaster informed me when I appeared on deck."

I knew not – and still know not - what to say. Have I somehow wandered into the plot of one of your novels?

"But," was all I could think to say, "but, if your servant is a spy of Fouché, mine is not necessarily in the pay of Talleyrand. What makes you think that she is?"

"Only that I cannot imagine Talleyrand allowing Fouché to set a spy upon us without also installing one of his own. And she did leave the ship with Pierrot this morning."

I had nothing to say to this, so I merely munched my cannolo. I dare say it was as delicious as Charles had pronounced it, but of the flavour I have no recollection whatever.

Words fail me to describe the smug smile with which Charles observed my reaction.

"Well?" he asked, at length, "Is it good? Do the famed cannoli of Genoa live up to their reputation?"

"How can be I expected to think of pastries after what you have just told me? You are as bad as Henry."

"I thank you for the compliment, my dear, but, really, I think we should be deciding what to do about these cuckoos in our nest, rather than sitting around wasting time in the discussion of Genoese delicacies, no matter how toothsome you may find them."

"I am of your sentiments exactly, but may I remind you that this halt for refreshment was your idea."

"I am glad to see that our sentiments coincide, my pet, and should hope that they will always do so. So, having pronounced these viands excellent of their sort, what shall we do now?"

"What do you propose? You have obviously

given the matter some thought while I have been intent on nothing but Kaffee-Kuchen."

"The excellence of which has assisted my cogitation considerably, you may be assured. What I propose is that we dismiss the offenders instantly, or rather, not quite instantly, but when they have served their purpose of conveying our bags from the ship. Tomorrow we will no doubt find ourselves assailed by no end of volunteers for the vacant positions. This will give us some idea of the extent of the French spy network in this city, for they will have been sent by their spymaster, you may have no doubt."

"But why should the French Government be interested in spying on us? I can see no sense in it."

"The French authorities need neither rhyme nor reason, though they will seize on either if available. It is enough that we stayed at the embassy. We are, therefore, in their eyes, spies, and must be watched constantly, either to gain information, or to prevent the outrages we are planning. Both Talleyrand and Fouché think far more of strengthening their own positions than of any danger to the Republic, and agents are cheap. But what I also propose is that on Monday we call upon these non-friends of yours, and see what we shall see. Depending on what we do see, what do you say to our Mr Thorpe as my valet-cum-private secretary, with his sister as your companion-cum-lady's maid?"

"Surely you cannot be serious in such a proposal?" I exclaimed.

"Why not? Think about it, my love. At least we could be sure that they are not French spies. Do you have any reason to think them incapable of performing such functions?"

"Other than my firm conviction that both Mr Thorpe and his sister are completely untrustworthy, and will only do whatever serves their own ends, and even that unwillingly, no."

"But this will serve their ends. It will provide some means of support, and it will get them out of Genoa. Is that not precisely what Mr Thorpe was asking for? Or do you think that they will sell us out to the French – for they will almost certainly be approached by them, once their position is known – that they will take Bonaparte's gold to betray their own countrymen?"

"I do not think them quite so lost to decency as

that, no. But it is so embarrassing, and so strange!"

"So it is. But we did not undertake the Grand Tour to encounter familiar subjects, did we? However, there is ample time for reflection before Monday, and we have a deal to do meanwhile, so may I suggest that we set about arranging lodgings instead of sitting around here indulging our beastly appetites? Not that I greatly wish to deprive you of that uneaten half of your cannolo, but it is a shame to waste it."

So we paid our call on the consul, and found a suite of rooms to suit, and played out the comedy with Pierrot and Suzette. And what a comedy it was, too, with all their pleadings and entreaties and crocodile tears.

Charles was very good at his part. He simply refused to hear their pleas and objections, and went on as if they had never occurred, wishing his faithful servants a prosperous return home, and promising them characters should they ever be in need of such assistance from him. They parted from us most unwillingly, but eventually left, with a strange mixture of sobs and imprecations such as only the French are capable of.

"Well," said Charles, when they had gone, "I did wonder whether to change lodgings now that they are out of the way, but concluded that would look too suspicious. However, we are now without servants until our new ones can be engaged, my dear. What a mercy it is that one of us has had some practice at acting as a lady's maid!"

Now that I have put all this down on paper, it seems more ridiculous than ever. I would believe anything of Messrs Fouché and Talleyrand, but I simply cannot persuade myself to believe that Mr Thorpe would make an adequate valet. Still less can I believe in Miss Thorpe as a lady's maid, even though I believe on the continent the post is held in rather more esteem than it is at home. Why is she even here in Genoa? Should she not be at home with her parents, not following her brother about Europe? Besides, there are circumstances, beyond her likely competence or lack thereof, that make her particularly unsuitable. Perhaps Charles is not aware of exactly what passed between Miss Thorpe and my brother Frederick last year. Well, for that matter, *I* do not know *exactly* what passed between them, but I know my brother, and I have a pretty fair idea of what he was after when he paid attentions to her, and

I should be very surprised to hear that he ceased those attentions before he had attained his end.

I really do not want to spend tomorrow arguing it all over again, but it looks as if there will be no alternative form of entertainment on offer.

Forgive me, my love. It has been a long, hot day, and my temporary-acting-tiring-woman is pressing for it to end. I will write again as soon as I may, and tell you how this riddle played itself out. Pray direct any letter you may send to me to Florence, for that is our next destination, and we shall be leaving this city as soon as may be.

As to the question you raise in your postscript, these things are looked upon in a much more relaxed light this side of the Alps. I agree, however, that it would be wiser to put more distance between us and Paris, and we shall be doing so as soon as may be.

Be sure, however that not a day passes without you and Henry occupying the thoughts of

Your dear friend

Eleanor

Letter the Twentieth : Miss Morland to Lady Hapworth, in Genoa

Fullerton

21st January 1803

Dear Eleanor,

I was so worried by the latest news from London when I wrote my last. How glad I am to hear that you are safe! And in Italy, too. How romantic! Genoa sounds just the sort of place for plots and feuds, quite like Romeo and Juliet. Oh, but that was Verona! Do you by any chance intend to go there while you are in Italy? How marvellous that would be! And Venice! Could anyone find more romantic a destination?

But I am ahead of myself, I see.

What a surprise it was to hear your news of the Thorpes! I hardly know what to say. Isabella and I were great friends in Bath, but I find it hard to forgive the way she treated my brother. But, then, she herself was treated even more shabbily by – but I see

I must not say any more here. How very embarrassing it all is!

Does your noble husband – I cannot quite bring myself to call him just Charles, as yet – does he know the full history of the brother and sister he proposes to engage? How should you feel, with Isabella as your servant? I never liked Mr Thorpe, and yet I should not like to think of him destitute in a foreign land, and this reluctance is strengthened when I think of his sister.

But you are so wise, and, from what you tell of him, your Charles – there, I have said it! – must be even more clever. I am sure that whatever you do it will be for the best.

It is all very quiet here at home, after the delights and excitement of Northanger Abbey, but at least we hear no more of the Honourable Lavinia. I could have no ease in her presence in the same house, though Henry assured me there was not the slightest danger, and invited me to contemplate the possibility that it might be the dowager herself in whom the General was interested on his own behalf, rather than her daughter as bait for his son.

"For you must consider," he said, "that my

father, though it is undoubtedly true that he gets no younger as time passes, is still a vigorous man and may be thinking of some consolation to his loneliness now that my sister has left him. I dare say "my wife, Lady Lumpton" sounds to his ears nearly as well as "my daughter, the viscountess." He has always been inclined to place too much emphasis on rank. I blame the military training, personally. Frederick is just the same."

I fear I am such a shy, timorous, self-doubting creature that I cannot be easy in the face of competition, not until a certain event takes place, that is. Until then, I still cannot really believe my own good fortune, however many times Henry reassures me.

I will write to you at Florence, as you say. Please lose no time in continuing your narration. It is selfish to ask, I know, but I am all agog to hear, and every letter from you greatly eases the heart of

    Your loving friend

    Catherine.

Letter the Twenty-First :   Lady Hapworth to Miss Morland

Florence

3rd February 1803

My very dear Catherine,

You must not undervalue yourself so. I know your worth, Henry knows your worth, I rather suspect that by now even my father is beginning to know your worth. Do you not think our opinions worthy of belief? And do you not see that even having the courage to stand up against them is proof that you are not such a timid soul as you would have us believe? Perhaps I am getting tangled in my logic there, but I think you will know what I mean. You are our own, dear Catherine. I am sure that only Henry can love you more than I do, and I am equally sure that he does. Such doubting and incredulity is unworthy of you, my dear. It is also unworthy of Henry and unworthy of me. Put it all behind you and look forward to the future.

I intend to look to the future as soon as may be,

but for the moment I have a little of the past to recount, as you have been good enough to express some little interest in our dealings with your old friends, Mr and Miss Thorpe.

We kept the appointment that my lord and master had made – I cannot bring myself to call him "my caro sposo", as I heard an English lady refer to her husband the other day in the *Uffizi*. I use the term 'lady' in the broadest sense, of course, such an affected person she was, with her airs and graces, and her whining, nasal tones and continual boasting of said 'sposo', who was, after all, no more than some sort of oily merchant and himself capable of conversing only about the charms of his "new house, at Maple Grove," and his "splendid new barouche-landau". She was so full of her own, miniscule self-importance that she made no bones about directly contradicting me when I pointed out that the bronze statue of the young David over whom she was pontificating was by Donatello, not Michelangelo, who made the large, marble statue outside the Signoria.

"You are mistaken, young lady," she replied. "I think you will find that the statue of David is by Michelangelo. I have often heard tell of

Michelangelo's David, but never of this other person."

It is people like that who give the English a bad name abroad. I wasted no more words on her, but I confess I gave in to temptation, and sent an attendant to fetch me a chair, just so that I could observe her face when he returned to announce in those carrying tones they all use –

"E pronta la portantina di Madama la Viscontessa!"

I was not disappointed by the look on her face, although I doubt if her Italian stretches to the word for Sedan chair. Viscontessa, however, can hardly be misunderstood.

Forgive me, my dear, all this is by way of putting off the evil day when I must confess to you our dealings with your friends the Thorpes.

Charles had made enquiries in the meantime, and expressed great reluctance to take me with him, but would give no reason other than he did not think it 'suitable'.

I am, however, far too aware of Charles' soft heart, and his susceptibility to female persuasion, and while perfectly sure of both his fidelity and his judgement, felt that I could not abandon him to the wiles of two such dubious characters without my presence and support. I therefore insisted, and he gave way with his customary good grace, although I could see that he was reluctant.

Mr Thorpe's description of his lodging as "but a stone's throw from here" had led me to expect a neighbourhood rather less unsavoury than that to which Charles now led me. We set off down the Strada Nuova, with all its magnificence, and turned off about halfway along onto the very next street. What a difference this made. Behind us, we had left an entire street of palaces: before us there stretched a scene of such squalor and dilapidation as I have never before witnessed. The crumbling stones and flaking plaster on all sides seemed to be held up only by the copious graffiti they bore, while the rotting wood of the ill-fitting doorways seemed almost to crumble before our eyes, and the filth covering the road surface challenged both eyes and nose to defy knowledge of its origin.

On the corner of every alley that led off from this thoroughfare, and they were numerous, stood female persons, of all ages from matrons to mere children, gesticulating and calling out to passers-by in dialect too thick to comprehend, and with gestures with which I was not familiar.

"What are all these women doing here?" I asked Charles.

"They are…. laying out their wares, I suppose," he replied. "Yes, that is it. They are street….. vendors, just as one sees all over the city."

"Street vendors?" I replied, in all my innocence. "But they have nothing to sell. Where is their merchandise?"

"Oh, they have plenty of the sort of merchandise that men come to the Via Maddalena to buy. See, just as in any other market, there will always be customers who insist on squeezing the fruit before they buy."

And he pointed to a roughly dressed labourer of some sort, who was feeling the person of one of these women in a most immodest fashion, before she took his hand and led him through one of the crumbling doors.

I felt my face reddening as I realized to what sort of place I had insisted on coming.

"Now," said Charles, "do you see why I wished you to stay behind? Do you wish us to return to our apartment now, my dear?"

I shook my head, for, I know not why, but it seemed to me unwise to betray any sort of weakness in this place.

"No, lead on," I said. "*That* you should wish to come here without me I can readily appreciate. *Why* you should wish to do so, however, is capable of at least two interpretations, and I should be very sorry even to consider the second of them. Let us get this over with, then."

After all this perturbation, the Angelo d'Oro proved to be no more villainous on the inside than many English inns I have been obliged to patronize in my time. In fact, with its clean floors, neat tables and welcoming matron at the bar, it seemed almost cosy by comparison with the street outside. I was almost as disappointed as you would have been, my dear, by my failure to observe a single sinister character sharpening a stiletto, or even a drunken brawl in a corner. I could not help having my doubts, however, about some of the female clientele chatting so animatedly to the clients of the opposite sex.

Madama had obviously been primed to expect the *Milord Inglese,* and led us straight up to the Thorpes' apartment. Here we were not disappointed of the expected squalor, the goodwill generated by the announcement of Signor Thorpe's great friends having evidently not stretched as far as extra credit. Never have I seen a more wretched set of rooms. The meanest farm labourer at Northanger lives far more comfortably. In fact the widows and derelicts of our tenants are looked after better. I am aware that this is not the case everywhere, however, and that my own life has been rather sheltered.

Mr Thorpe greeted us with such expressions of grateful delight as the most self-satisfied of mortals would find hard to credit, while his sister was determined not to be outdone.

Charles, however, cut short these protestations, seating himself at the rickety table with his pocket book before him, while I took the other chair, so that the hosts must perforce stand to reply to their guests' enquiries.

"Let us be clear how we stand," he said. "I gather that you are both seeking gainful employment and a means of leaving this city."

Mr Thorpe began a rambling explanation of their circumstances, but was again cut short.

"I assume," said Charles, "that a prerequisite of your departure will be the payment of certain debts."

This time, after confirming my darling's guess, Thorpe began to list the amounts outstanding to various tradesmen.

"All that can be settled later," interrupted Charles, "depending on whether I decide to offer you employment. I tell you now, I may have a vacancy for the sort of factotum you appear to be offering yourself as, and my wife may have a similar position she may be prepared to offer to Miss Thorpe, but so far I have seen nothing to induce me to make such an offer. If you wish me to do so, you must persuade me."

"Before you attempt to do so, perhaps you would be so good as to call for some coffee and cannoli, and perhaps Miss Thorpe would like to show Lady Hapworth her own accommodation, where they can discuss both old times and new, while we do business,"

Normally I should have objected to such

exclusion, to being relegated to a mere female adjunct, but this was all pre-concerted, and I had my own part to play. So I allowed Miss Thorpe to conduct me into her own particular garret and to sit me on the one wobbly chair which, apart from the narrow bed and a curtain across one corner, formed the entire furniture of the room.

At first she was inclined to reminisce about "those darling days in Bath last year, and what fun we all had together, you and I and your delightful brother and that curious little girl, Catherine Morland", but I took a leaf from Charles' book, and brought her up with –

"Before you go on to say anything more about Miss Morland, I had better point out, Miss Thorpe, that Miss Morland is shortly to be my sister. She will be Mrs Henry Tilney as soon after my return to England as can be managed."

At this she turned to all delight on the part of "dear, dear Catherine, such a friend she was to me, and she might have been my sister too, you know, Miss Tilney, that is to say, your ladyship," and similar expressions of gratification.

Those, too, I curtailed.

"Miss Thorpe," I said, "I understand that you place your hopes of escaping from your creditors here in Genoa on obtaining a position in what might be considered by the natives as my 'retinue', and that you are offering yourself in the position of lady's companion. Let us be clear with one another from the outset. I neither need nor desire a lady's companion. I am on my honeymoon, and the only companion I require is my husband, who fills the position perfectly. My husband has been frank with your brother. Permit me to be equally blunt with you. If I did desire such a companion, you would not be my first choice, no, nor my second, third, or thirty-third neither."

At this she cast herself upon the bed, and began to writhe and moan in a fashion quite as extravagant as any of your heroines, athough I could not quite make out the volume which was evidently her inspiration, so that I was obliged to enforce moderation.

"Calm yourself, Miss Thorpe. Such behaviour does not increase my respect for you. I am, however, naturally reluctant to abandon any countrywoman in distress in foreign parts, especially one with whom, in former days, I have been on terms of what might be called intimacy, even though only such an intimacy as might spring up at a watering place and be forgotten after a fortnight at home. I am therefore prepared to consider your proposal, but there are points on which I must first be satisfied. The first of these is how you came to be travelling the continent with your brother. Should you not be still in England with your mother and sisters?"

"Oh, my lady, you should know as well as I why things could not go on as they had before. When your bro….. that is to say, when news of my misfortune became generally known in Bath, it was impossible for us to continue there. My mother cast me out, told me I was no longer her daughter, forbade me her company and that of my sisters. I wept and besought her, but she was as adamant. She would not, she said, allow my sisters' chances to be ruined by my disgrace, and would forever hold me out to them as a dreadful example of the fate that might befall them. There was a young parson paying his addresses to Amelia at the time, and I believe she felt she must adopt such a course.

That was a very hard time for me. The only person who stood by me was my brother. He took me in, paid for the necessary operation, and looked after me in the fever that followed. But then it came to light that John's payment had only been a deposit. An extra bill was tendered, with threats of exposure to the magistrates. We could not pay, and dare not take the risk.

Had the peace not fallen in just then, I know not what we should have done. A friend of John's was taking a a party to France on his yacht, and offered us passage out of the country. We were set down at Boulogne at low tide, carried through the surf on the backs of those half women- half beasts of burden who make their living by landing passengers so. Since then, we have made shift to live on very little money, moving on from town to town when we could no longer maintain our credit. Now you see us quite at the end of our resources, and if you do not help us we must soon perish. I beg you, Miss Tilney, that is to say, my lady, take pity on us. For the sake of old times, when I, too, might have been your sister if – but I see I must not speak of such things – for the sake of old times, give us a chance to earn our living in your service."

To tell you the truth, Catherine dear, this last reference both deterred me from any further contact with these people, and at the same time awoke feelings of obligation. Isabella Thorpe *had* been treated very shabbily by my brother Frederick and my warnings to her at the time had been but lukewarm. I felt it incumbent on me to make up in some way as best I could for my brother's selfishness. But to admit as much would never do, for we had determined among ourselves to show no weakness towards our supplicants from the very beginning.

"Well, well," I said, "you have had misfortunes, that I will not deny. But whether we can help you or not must be my husband's decision. Shall we rejoin the gentlemen and see how they have gone on?"

They had, it appeared, gone on well enough.

Charles raised an eyebrow at me as we entered the other room, and I nodded, I hope imperceptibly to all but him. Both Thorpes had their backs to me at the time, so the assumption was not unreasonable.

"Well," said he, "it appears that we are in agreement. So, Miss Thorpe, I am prepared to assist you both on terms which your brother has already agreed. There is wanting only your agreement before I speak to your principal creditor, who is, I believe, your landlord here. Should you wish these terms to be explained to you."

"Thank you, my lord, but if my brother has expressed his consent, then I am happy to follow his example."

"Very well. I shall put arrangements in train. The mariners promise me a *tramontana* on Wednesday. If they are right, we shall be sailing on the *San Lorenzo* at daybreak. Be sure to present yourselves betimes, or we shall leave without you. I need hardly remind you that if we are obliged to do so, none of the payments we have discussed this morning will be made. Good day to you, Miss Thorpe, Mr Thorpe."

I saw very little of Charles for the rest of the day, while he arranged with the Genoese bankers about the complicated series of payments that were to be made on receipt of further instructions from him.

It all seems to me to be a great deal of trouble and expense for very little advantage, but, then, nothing is too much trouble and expense for dear Charles if he thinks it will please me. I am far from sure that it *will* please me, but, as Charles puts it, they are not particularly wanted on the voyage, and if they do not turn up we will have lost nothing but a little time and trouble, and gained the inestimable satisfaction of knowing that we have done our charitable duty towards old acquaintances in distress.

That will be a comfort to my mind, I am sure, but not nearly so much comfort as relating all this to you has been, my dear.

Forgive me for such a long letter on a not very pleasant subject. I will make up for it by relating all the delights of Florence in my next.

I begin to wonder whether all this travel is such a very good thing. It was different when we were in Paris. One could grow accustomed to things there, but this vagabond existence does not suit me. Charles is already talking about moving on to Rome, however.

I promise to be more cheerful next time, and to write you such a letter as will make you proud of

Your loving sister,

Eleanor.

Letter the Twenty-Second : Miss Morland to Lady Hapworth, in Florence

Fullerton

14th February 1803

Dear, dear Eleanor,

How I long for the day when you can truly be my sister. Is it such a very bad fate to consider returning home to? I own that I cannot help but fear a much worse one for you both if you dally on the continent much longer.

Mr Allen brought us news this morning of Bonaparte's latest speech in the French parliament –

"In London there are two factions struggling for power; one of them has made peace, the other has sworn implacable hatred to France. While this partisan strife lasts, the Republic must take precautions. Half a million must be ready to defend and avenge her. Alone, England can never resist her."

Everyone one meets is very much changed

from the mood in which we greeted the peace only last year.

Bonaparte has broken his word to us too often, and I fear it cannot be long before we see redcoats marching through the streets again, and press gangs scouring the ports.

You will laugh, and say that I am only repeating what Henry has told me, and I understand why you would do so. You are so brave, and so clever, and surrounded, I make no doubt, by clever people who tell you there is nothing to fear, but you cannot know what the feeling is like here. If war does break out again, what will you and your husband do, so far away from home, with so many hostile leagues to traverse before you can get back?

You may be right, and I am only being my old, timorous self, expecting Gothick horrors on all sides when the worst that is likely to happen to you is a touch of the sun. But consider the alternatives, I beg you, my dear, and find it possible to think yourself mistaken.

There, now I have got that out of my system, and may be comfortable again, and ask sensible questions. How are you getting on with the Thorpes?

Never mind the delights of Florence. I have never seen them and am never likely to, whereas the Thorpes are a known quantity, as I believe the mathematicians say. It must be very embarrassing for you to have to deal with them every day, and so intimately too. I cannot imagine that either of them would prove trustworthy in even the most menial tasks, and I am sure that your dealings with them must partake much more of the nature of an act of charity than you care to admit.

Of course I am sorry for what happened to poor Isabella. It is a subject on which it is difficult to speak, for an unmarried girl, at least, and it is made no easier by the fact that the person who would otherwise be cast as the villain of the piece is your brother. But she had herself only recently behaved very badly towards *my* brother, and while I wish her no particular ill, I find it difficult to be sympathetic. My feelings towards Mr Thorpe are similar.

It is but further proof of how much more noble your nature is than mine that you should assist them so.

We are very dull here, just now, the snow and the vicious gales preventing almost every excursion.

Mr Allen has taken to coming over only every other day, and Henry is quite frozen through when he arrives from Northanger. I have considered suggesting that he suspend his visits until the weather moderates, but have not yet found the courage to do so. At least the North winds are unfavourable for an invasion fleet to cross the channel. I know I must not think of such things, but that is all anyone is talking about these days.

    I drop hints now and then that perhaps mama might like to take Sally and me on a visit to Woodston, so that she might see the house that will be my home after the great day, but she remains resolutely deaf to all pleas.

    As you must to mine, my dear Eleanor, You are on the spot, you are older and wiser than I, and in the care of one wiser still, if I am to believe your descriptions, and you must be much better placed to form an opinion of the risk of staying in Italy than I ever could.

    Write soon, and ease the girlish fears of

    Your loving friend

    Catherine

Letter the Twenty-Third :   **Lady Hapworth**
to Miss Morland

Florence

28th February 1803

Dear Catherine,

Pray do not be concerned for us. The noises you hear in England from our friend in Paris receive but pale echoes this side the Alps. I spoke to the Grand Duke himself the other day, and he assured me there was no need for alarm. The treaty with the French guarantees the safety and sovereignty of the Grand Duchy, and I need have no fear for the efficacy of his protection.

I only wish one did not see so many French troops on the streets here. Surely they cannot all be on leave and visiting the already plundered galleries?

We went together yesterday to the *Uffizi*, and what a sight it was! I had popped in previously, just for a quick look, while Charles was busy with his bankers – you remember, I mentioned that awful Mrs

Duckling or whatever her name was. Charles had been right round the gallery in days gone by, and was horrified. Practically every second picture was gone, and all of the great masterpieces he had been wishing to show me. The walls, half bare, made but a sorry sight, and gave little indication of how things must have been.

The sculptures had fared rather better. Perhaps a painting, which can be rolled up and stored in a tube if necessary, is more suitable for plunder than a heavy, rigid piece of bronze or marble.

But there is a great deal about Florence that even the French army were unable to spoil. The view from the hilltop at Fiesole is quite as spectacular as it is reputed to be. Henry could, perhaps, provide all the technical terms to describe its picturesqueness, and Charles attempted to impress a few of them on me, but all I could think of was that all the stolen pictures could scarcely equal this miraculous vista. So inadequate is the hand of man compared with that of God!

By comparison with Genoa, the buildings here are rather less decrepit, and the streets are much cleaner. They are, however, every bit as crowded, if not more so.

Charles seems to know all sorts of people here, and we are never short of an evening out. He, of course, is in his element with his perfect, Tuscan Italian, and much sought after. I try to give as good as I get in the way of *conversazioni,* but I very soon tire of the effort. Fortunately, one meets other English people almost everywhere one goes, which provides ample leisure, not only from the constant effort of *parlando Italiano*, but also to remember why we did not choose to spend our honeymoon in Bath or Buxton or Brighton. I would happily exchange every Englishwoman in Florence for an hour's quiet converse with you, my dear.

As for your friends the Thorpes, we get on better than I expected, having sat on them thoroughly at first meeting. I see very little of the brother, whom Henry keeps busy on all sorts of mysterious tasks, mostly involving messages to his friends here. Isabella is, as you suspected, very little use as a lady's maid, although I have not quite given up all hope of training her to suit me. She is, however of great utility as a dogsbody and punching bag.

I do not mean that last phrase literally, of

course, although I sometimes wonder, but I do begin to perceive the desirability of having someone else to do all the tedious little jobs and errands that come up from time to time that one does not care to entrust to a servant at an inn, and the even greater desirability of having an object on which one can vent one's temper and frustration when things go wrong.

I have never seen the point of having a lady's companion before, but having tried one, I am quite converted to the practice. It is not a position I should like to occupy myself, however.

We go to Pisa tomorrow, to view the famous leaning tower. Unless it falls upon me, you shall hear all about it soon from

Your very dear friend,

Eleanor.

Letter the Twenty-Fourth : Miss Morland to Lady Hapworth, in Florence

Woodston

14th March 1803

Dear Eleanor,

Henry has brought me to see the new additions and decorations he has made to the parsonage here. I could not resist writing to you while I could put the superscription above. It is all a sell, however, as I shall have to finish this when I get back home, for the days are not yet so long and we must leave soon.

Soon, however, I shall not have to get back home while the light lasts, for this will *be* my home. I cannot describe to you the feelings this thought conjures up in me, but I dare say you know what I mean. Do you not find the delights of the continent pale, and the thoughts of home grow sweeter?

The parsonage is a splendid house, and the alterations and decorations Henry has made to it are perfectly charming. Apart from the front and back parlours, the dining room, the hall and the bedrooms, very little will need to be done to it to make it a delightful place to spend our married life in.

You do realize, do you not, that the date from which that married life will commence is entirely dependent upon you? Both my parents continually urge me to "get on with it", and even Henry occasionally lets slip the odd sign of impatience. Your father, however, does not join in the chorus, which sometimes makes me wonder if he does not still place his hopes in the Honourable Lavinia, or some other scion of the nobility.

Meanwhile, the news of the hostile forces gathering in the ports of northern France and the Low Countries which was read out in the King's message to Parliament last week has set us all in a flurry again. You say that you are in no danger, and of course I must believe you, but I cannot help but worry.

The life you are leading sounds very exciting, my dear, seeing all those romantic places and meeting so many famous people, but I do not think I should like it, any more than in real life I should like to be kidnapped by banditti or bricked up in a tower. And yet, just a year ago, all my hopes and dreams were filled with such images. I must be getting old, alas.

But at least I may not die an old maid quite yet and the thought of creating a new home at Woodston has me more excited than I can describe. But fear not, my friend, I am quite reconciled to the thought that it shall not be just yet, and I give you leave to enjoy your foreign jaunts to the full, so long as you never forget to recount them to

Your steadfast friend,

Catherine.

P.S.

Isabella Thorpe as a dogsbody and punching bag sounds a very good idea to me. I hope your Charles is treating John to the same medicine.

Letter the Twenty-Fifth : Lady Hapworth to Miss Morland

Florence

1st April 1803

Dear Catherine,

Pisa was a washout. The Leaning Tower looks quite excessively precarious, and both Charles and I declined positively to engage in climbing it. We had just started to walk around the famous *Campo dei Miracoli* when our calm was shattered by a tremendous thunderclap. The rain continued all day, and we spent the rest of our time cowering in the baptistery for shelter, as there was a popish service going on in the cathedral. As soon as there was a momentary halt, we had to wade to our carriage and make shift to dry ourselves as best we could on the way back to Florence. These Italian cities are built on the assumption that it will never rain. Their streets have no drainage, and so, when it does rain, they become rushing watercourses, ankle deep. Their marble pavements, so impressive to look at normally, turn to slippery deathtraps when wet, and we counted ourselves lucky to get back to our carriage.

We leave this place tomorrow. I wish I could tell you it is for Leghorn to take ship home, but if I did the only excuse for doing so would be the date.

The recall of poor Lord Whitworth from Paris, and of the French ambassador from London has, I admit it, frightened me at last. Coupled with the news we have here of French Troops gathering on the borders of both Tuscany and the Papal States, I fear that your timidity, as you choose to call it, may soon prove more timely than all our so-called courage and wisdom.

In fact, we are moving on to Rome. Charles, I fear, is absolutely inexhaustible in his quest for antiquities and art treasures. The fact that most of them have been stolen by the French merely spurs him on. For myself, I should have been happy to come straight home from Paris, but I cannot bear to spoil his enthusiasm, especially when he urges it so persuasively, in ways that modesty forbids me to describe to an unmarried woman.

I fear I have no time just now to divagate

further upon the sights of Florence, but I cannot deny you my latest report on our old friends from Bath.

Isabella, I have discovered, is quite a fair hand at sewing, and I have set her to all the mending that I have been putting off for weeks. She takes this with a much better grace than some of the tasks I have given her. I dare say she is accustomed to doing something similar at home.

She will insist on chattering on as she does her work, as if we were still but common acquaintances at Bath, but when we are at home, as it were, this can be countenanced. I never intended her to wait on table, or clean the floors. We have inn servants for that sort of thing, after all, and I take care that she is never included in any invitations we receive.

John Thorpe's knowledge of horseflesh seems to have improved no end since the useless nag he had at Bath. At any rate we have never lacked for serviceable beasts to pull our carriage, or to ride out upon, since he took service with us. Perhaps it was not so much expertise he was lacking as ready money?

Both are rather plumper now than when first met them in Genoa, and seem disposed to be grateful for the relief, however conditional, that they have received.

Let us hope they will continue so.

Let us hope, too, that it will not now be so very long before you see the rather tanned face of

Your loving sister,

Eleanor.

Letter the Twenty-Sixth :   Viscount Hapworth to Mr Henry Tilney

Florence

5th April 1803

Dear Henry,

I wish you could persuade your sister to come home. This is not to say that I have any criticism of her character or of her conduct. Both are completely beyond reproach. It is their very excellence that poses problems.

She is quite tireless and utterly fearless in her pursuit of knowledge, where it is clear that she cannot bear being outdone by anyone, even her own husband. She will hear none of my hints about the worsening situation in Europe, nor see any of the signs of the armies mustering for what must shortly be another conflagration.

It was with the utmost difficulty that I dragged

her away from Paris, and now that we are in Italy she is determined to "finish the grand tour."

I point out that, as far as art treasures and antiquities go, everything that has not been nailed down – and a large portion of those that *were* nailed down – has already been stolen by the French, and is in the Louvre, or some General's palace, but this will not do. She must see what is left, and lament over the blank spaces, and hunt about for acceptable substitutes.

I have already invented several excuses for moving her further from the despotic power, but it is slow, oh, so slow, progress.

We leave for Rome tomorrow, and I hope to move on from there as soon as may be, to Naples, where there will be comparative safety, if any is to be found in Italy. You may write in the meantime to the embassy in Rome, where I shall be making an early call on our arrival there.

Could not your father be struck by some mysterious wasting disease, and be calling out for his daughter from his deathbed, or some such? Or you yourself be in urgent need of a consultation on some mysterious family matter that cannot be dealt with, or even revealed, by correspondence? You will know better than I what might induce your sister to return early, and I beg you to use any means. You know the general nature of the missions I sometimes undertake for Lord Castlereagh, and can appreciate that I have sources of information I may not reveal. Those sources make me very uneasy with our situation here, and the news from France and England is not encouraging. I should be very surprised if the present peace lasts the summer, and I have no desire to involve my wife in a headlong flight from "*La Grande Armée*".

Any help you could give would greatly ease the heart of

Your anxious brother,

Hapworth

Letter the Twenty-Seventh : Mr Henry Tilney to Lord Hapworth, in Rome

Woodston

12 April 1803

My Dear Hapworth,

Barring a few hours, you have known my sister quite as long as I have. If you have ever found her amenable to reason once she has made her mind up then you have done more than I.

However, I will take the matter up, and do what I can.

You may find this difficult to believe, but I am so old-fashioned as to be rather fond of my only sister, and the idea of her, and even you, in a French prison does not greatly appeal to me.

Eleanor is the most dutiful of creatures, and, perhaps, her conscience may be worked on when her reason cannot.

I have no more than a germ of an idea as to how I may accomplish what you ask, and the only way I can think of is sorely against my conscience as a clergyman, but I shall see what I can do.

I know I can rely upon you to second whatever suggestion I may come up with, and perhaps the two of us may induce her to do the sensible thing for once.

Never let it be said that sister- no, nor brother of mine – were ever let down by

Your dependable brother,

Henry Tilney

Letter the Twenty-Eighth : Mr Henry Tilney to Lady Hapworth, in Rome

Northanger

14th April 1803

My very dear Eleanor,

Permit me to repress all envious thoughts that inevitably arise when I contemplate the two of you strolling through the Forum, and clambering among the very seats of the Colosseum itself, and to wish you joy of your stay in the eternal city.

Joy, I fear is in but short supply here. Our father had a bad fall while hunting last week, and has not woken since. The doctors give us no hopes other than that this condition could continue some while before the inevitable end.

But, forgive me, my dear, I am called to his side just now.

Later –

I have no very good news to report, I fear. He

was stirring in his coma, and crying out for you, my pet.

I sent immediately for the doctor, but he only shook his head and said that your presence might perhaps provide the stimulus required for his patient to regain consciousness. Otherwise, there is no hope.

I should not dream of suggesting that you cut short your enjoyment of your holiday by one minute on my own account, dear sister, but if you wish to see your parent again before the end, you may think of considering an early return.

I will send news of any change as soon as may be.

Until then, be sure that you are never far from the thoughts of

Your devoted brother,

Henry

Letter the Twenty-Ninth : Miss Morland to Lady Hapworth, in Rome

Fullerton

16th April 1803

Dear, dear Eleanor,

How I missed you last night when we all had dinner at Northanger Abbey to celebrate my birthday.

Your father was quite in his old form, every bit as archaically formal and fulsome in his complements when we arrived as when I first knew him. He even repeated the same comments about Mr Allen's dining room and carriage, as if he were still thinking of me as heir to the Fullerton estate.

I could almost have believed that John Thorpe had been spreading his old rumours again did I not know that he was otherwise- and elsewhere- engaged. By the way, I have not mentioned your encounter with the Thorpes to any one here, not even Henry. If you ask me why, I shall not be able to tell you, for I have no very clear idea myself. It is something to do with not wishing to remind anyone of James's disappointment, and something to do with natural reticence and something to do with I know not what. It just seemed better not to mention them.

James's disappointment, by the way, looks like to be soon mended. He is now seeing a great deal of an attorney's daughter at Oxford, reputed to have ten thousand pounds of her own. I am sure she must have more than those particular ten thousand attractions to draw James's notice, but I have never met her yet.

After dinner, General Tilney unbent so far as to canvas the possibility of his visiting us at Fullerton, a place where I never expected him to condescend to set his august foot. I have never seen him so generally complaisant and accommodating. I know great men can be whimsical, and may welcome you one day and warn you off the next, but I begin to believe he is reconciled to the match at last.

He seemed in the best of health –indeed, he boasted of it, and joked with my father upon his touch of gout.

All this pleased me very much, but what has delighted me even more has been the passing of this news on to you. After such a long absence, hearing that he is well and in good spirits must be such a comfort to you.

Do tell me all about Rome. Is it really full of wicked friars set on kidnapping English girls and forcing them to abjure their protestant faith? Are there ruins on every corner, and catacombs full of the bones and skeletons of the martyrs? Is St. Peter's really so very big?

All these details and more, I fear, will make very little headway in filling up the bottomless ignorance of

Your loving but unlearned sister,

Catherine

P.S.

I astonished the entire company by playing that Mozart you sent me on the great piano at Northanger. Henry was particularly impressed. I cannot thank you enough for your kindness.

Letter the Thirtieth : Lady Hapworth to Miss Morland

Rome

22nd April 1803

Dearest Catherine,

I was very glad to receive your latest, which enabled me to resolve some doubts I may have had in my mind.

Your news of my father's general well-being and of his improved state of mind towards you ease my mind more than you can know. I wish nothing more than a continued improvement in both.

Meanwhile, for the impression that the Eternal City makes on anyone with any pretence at education, I can only refer you to Mr Gibbon -

"My temper is not very susceptible of enthusiasm, and the enthusiasm which I do not feel I have ever scorned to affect. But, I can neither forget nor express the strong emotions which agitated my mind as I first approached and entered the eternal

city. After a sleepless night, I trod, with a lofty step, the ruins of the Forum; each memorable spot where Romulus stood, or Tully spoke, or Caesar fell, was at once present in my eye; and several days of intoxication were lost or enjoyed before I could descend to a cool and minute investigation."

I should hate to have to listen to what he would have to say when *overcome* by enthusiasm if this is an example of his absence of it, but he does express very well the sensations that overwhelm one at the discovery that one is actually in the Rome that one has heard so much about, the bugbear of our childhood, and the envy of all cities for an age or more.

It is true that there is no shortage of ruins here such as might inspire the most naïve as well as the most erudite, and of course all of them are positively stuffed with bones, skeletons and friars, but I must beg you to excuse me for the moment, as I have a particular task to do which exercises my mind so much at the moment that I find myself unable to concentrate on anything else.

Do not be alarmed, my dear, it is nothing of any consequence, and will never affect our friendship, but -you know how it is – sometimes a minor problem will so occupy one's mind that nothing can be done until it is dealt with.

I will write to you properly very soon.

Until then, be sure of the continued devotion of

Your sister

Eleanor.

Letter the Thirty-First :   Lady Hapworth to Mr Henry Tilney

Rome

22nd April 1803

Dear Henry,

I was most perturbed to read the news you sent me in your last letter, especially as in the same post there came a letter from our dear Catherine, who tells me that she and all her family had dinner with my father at Northanger the night after this disastrous fall, and that he was in full health and good spirits throughout the evening and saw them off the following morning.

I rejoice, naturally, at such a miraculous recovery, and consequently feel under no pressing obligation to shorten my honeymoon in order to hasten yours.

If you wanted me to come home early so that you and Catherine could marry the sooner, why did you not just say so?

I should have been perfectly happy to oblige, and, although I have not discussed the situation with him, I should be surprised if Charles felt differently.

As it is, I shall have no compunction about accepting Prince Borghese's invitation to Tivoli for the coming week, and we shall make up our minds what to do thereafter when the occasion arises.

Rest assured that in any case you will be kept informed of her movements by

Your wandering sister,

Eleanor

Letter the Thirty-second : Mr Henry Tilney to Lady Hapworth, in Rome

Woodston

14th May 1803

Dear Eleanor,

I admit the harmless subterfuge in which you have detected me, but make no apologies for attempting to save you from what I, and your husband, saw as your own willfulness.

For you must realize that my attempted deception was at your husband's instigation. He has long been troubled by the worsening international relations between our country and France, and would have returned home sooner but for your insistence on continuing your tour, which he did not have the heart to deprive you of. But now that you are each aware of the other's true feelings, I beg you to come home as soon as you can. Our father has it from his friends in the Horse Guards that all French ships in ports in the United Kingdom are shortly to be impounded. In the present state of affairs between the two countries, war must surely follow almost instantly.

Imagine the consequences of being left at the mercy of the Corsican Tyrant, which even you must concede to be a fate not to be recommended.

Can you not see that war must soon come? As soon as it does, Bonaparte will gobble up the rest of Italy, and your Concordat will make little or no difference. Rome is sure to be first on his list. As civilians, you and your husband should be in no immediate danger, but your position is bound to be most uncomfortable, and can only get worse as the blockade continues and specie can no longer be transmitted abroad.

I beg you, my darling sister, come home now, before it is too late. My father joins me in this plea, as does your brother Frederick, your friend Catherine and every one who loves and values you.

If you ask your Charles, you will find that he joins in the plea too.

Come home dear sister, and ease the hearts of all who value you, but especially that of

Your loving brother,

Henry.

Letter the Thirty-Third : Lady Hapworth to Miss Morland

Rome

22nd May 1803

Dearest Catherine,

I write this in the most urgent haste. French troops are reported marching on Rome from Ancona.

We leave within the hour for Civitavecchia, in the hope of finding a ship to England, or Gibraltar, or Malta, or anywhere out of Bonaparte's reach. If we cannot do so, then we must try the road to Naples. If any Italian state can stand against the French it must be the Regno, even if only for a while, and that while may give us to time to find passage to safety. Perhaps Bonaparte will delay at swallowing a gnat of such size with all the others.

Ignore what I just said about Civitavecchia . Mr Thorpe has just this minute arrived with news that war has been declared, that the road to Civitavecchia is barred, and that Napoleon has ordered the arrest of all British citizens within France and the Italian Republic. This is far too close for anything resembling comfort, and how bitterly I now regret not having made my desire to return home clear to Charles sooner.

Whatever will this man do next, if innocent civilians are now to be treated as enemies to be rounded up like cattle, and incarcerated?

You were right all along, my dear, and my deprecation of your fears was but vainglory. Well, I am paid for that now, and can only hope that it will not cost us dearer yet.

Forgive me, Catherine, I must go. There is so much to do and so little time. Write to me at Naples, if you will, and pray that your letter will soon be read there by

Your anxious sister,

Eleanor

Letter the Thirty-Fourth : Miss Morland to Lady Hapworth, in Naples

Fullerton

22nd May 1803

Dear, dear Eleanor,

How I do hope this letter finds you safe and well! The alarm which your last occasioned quite caused me to cry out while reading it, and your plight became the sensation of all the family. We are all excessively perturbed for your safety, and now have no compunction in uniting to beg you to come home as soon as may be, whatever your own inclinations may be.

Henry is the only one among us who does not appear at all anxious. He assures me, repeatedly, that if there is any Italian state that might cause Bonaparte to delay his plans, it is Naples, and reminds me that, although the French took the city in the year ninety-nine, they were soon driven out again.

That is a consolation, to be sure, but I for one had much sooner you were not involved in any such events. Besides, I rather think that Henry only affects insouciance in the hope of calming my anxiety, and that underneath his façade he is every bit as distraught as the rest of us.

We pray for your safe return every night. Please, write soon, and ease the heart of

Your loving friend,

Catherine

Letter the Thirty-Fifth : Lady Hapworth to Miss Morland

Naples

10th June 1803

My very dear Catherine,

What a tale I have to tell! You would scarce believe it if you read it in one of your novels.

Before that, however, let me thank you for your latest letter. That sheet of paper, with the familiar hand upon it, was the most welcome thing, bar one, that I have laid eyes upon in the past two weeks. I will tell you of the other anon.

You will be agog to hear all about Naples, and I know I cannot expect you to have any but the faintest interest in the trials and tribulations we had to undergo to get here. But forgive me, my dear, 'out of a full heart the mouth speaks', and I must just bore you with a short account of our travels.

At first all went well. Once we had passed the *Porta San Sebastiano*, we positively bowled along the Appian Way. We might have bowled along it to

Capua and safety, or even to take ship at Brindisi or Otranto itself. Yes, *that* Otranto, of the eponymous castle. I can hear you squeaking as you read this even now.

But, however, it was not to be. We had scarcely passed the tomb of Caecilia Metella when Mr Thorpe, who had ridden on ahead to survey the route, came back at a brisk canter, to inform us that the road ahead was blocked by French troops, who had, apparently, already almost encircled the city.

Mr Thorpe, by the way, behaved very creditably throughout our adventure, and I cannot speak too highly of his conduct while we were in peril. I would not quite go so far as to pronounce him to be a reformed character, but I believe the stimulus of danger may have roused him from his customary self-indulgence and lethargy. This, now I come to think of it, has given me an idea, but I will leave it for now and not interrupt my narrative.

We had perforce to take to the country roads, with which none of us were familiar, and although Charles did his best with his pocket compass, which he had providentially – or more likely, prudentially – brought with him, by sunset we were hopelessly lost.

We stumbled on and at last came to a clearing that housed a rude hut, apparently occupied by charcoal burners.

Imagine my surprise when Charles addressed them in a rough, barely comprehensible dialect similar to that they themselves employed. I have known for a long while that my husband is fluent in Italian when he wishes to be, and also that he had, as he put it, "knocked around Italy quite a bit" both before and after his banishment from Northanger, but I had never dreamed that his familiarity with the country might reach so far. Considering that for most of the period we were at war, I begin to wonder exactly how my beloved did spend that time.

Whatever he said seemed to suffice, at any rate, for his interlocutors produced bread and cheese and sausage, and flagons of rough wine, and we all sat down and engaged in animated conversation. That is to say that Charles and the peasants conversed very amicably while the rest of us gaped and yawned, and caught, perhaps, one word in ten.

After it had become full dark, our hosts were inclined to sleep, having no light but the moon and their banked up fire.

Miss Thorpe was disposed to make difficulties about where we should spend the night, but Charles would have none of it. Under his direction a serviceable bed was built up inside the landaulette with cushions and rugs, which was consigned to the ladies, while the gentlemen lay on the ground with their cloaks over them, like their Roman counterparts.

A spring night under the moon and stars in Italy sounds very romantic, does it not? It is not quite as romantic as it sounds, my dear, but neither is it any great hardship. The worst thing about it was the constant wriggling and squirming of my bedfellow, but even she subsided at last.

It was just as well the hardship was not too great, for we had many more such nights ahead of us.

Charles explained it all to me in the morning, when I took my turn with him on the box.

"You may have gathered, my love," he began, "that this is not my first visit to these parts…."

"I assure you, my darling, the thought would never have occurred to me, especially considering your apparent familiarity with everywhere we go, the old acquaintances we continually meet, and your fluency – which you take great pains to conceal except in the direst need - in all sorts of obscure dialects."

"Well, my Lady Sarcasm, your omniscience, perhaps, includes the knowledge that for a long time now I have been undertaking confidential missions on behalf of certain persons in Government…"

"Acting the glorified errand boy, I know. And I do glorify thee for it. I will happily glorify you at a moment's notice, in any role, you know that."

"Well, I have not been acting, as is generally supposed, for my cousin, the late Viscount, but for Lord Castlereagh, mostly in the south of Italy."

"Our present hosts are carbonari, which is not just to say charcoal-burners. They wander the country, to a degree, cutting wood and making charcoal for sale in the neighbouring towns. There are many thousands of them, spread across the peninsula in bands like this one. They keep in touch with one another, take messages, spread news, look out for one another. They are not quite a secret society, but not far off."

"They have been useful to me in the past, and

last year I was able to be useful to them, in such a way that has left them quite inordinately grateful. They know all the secret ways and paths long forgotten by others, and they will guide us by them until we are out of danger."

"How you intrigue me, my darling! I positively long to hear all about this great service which has given rise to so much gratitude."

"Forgive me, dearest, the secret is not mine to reveal. What I can reveal, however, is this, which our guide presented to me last night. You may care to read it. I make no doubt your Italian is more than adequate, and, if not, there is a French translation at the bottom."

'This' turned out to be a crumpled handbill, crudely printed with many points of exclamation, offering a reward for information leading to the apprehension of *"I due Hapworti"*, a pair of notorious English spies, wanted by the French authorities for committing numerous "atrocities and acts of terrorism", with the usual sort of description that might apply to anyone.

"I pondered a long while over whether to show you this," said Charles, when I looked up from my reading. "But I decided that you need to know just how much danger we are in. If we fall into the wrong hands, the lives of "the two Hapworths" will not be worth two ha'porth of the polenta you had for breakfast, my dear."

"Very amusing, I am sure. As for the rest, you will tell me one day, I dare say. But meanwhile our guides seem to be at a stand."

For we had halted by the ruins, or rather wreckage of a crude wooden bridge that had spanned the watercourse with which we were now confronted. Our guides, it appeared, had not been this way for a while, and were not expecting this obstacle. They stood around, gossiping and gesticulating in a particularly Italian way, until one of them came back and addressed Charles.

Of what he had to say, I caught only two words "*mal aria*", which I took to mean bad air. It turned out that they thought the water should be fordable, but were reluctant to enter it for fear of the bad air arising from it. It was not, of course, that they feared for themselves, but they did not wish the "*belle donne Inglesi*" to catch the fever which so often arose from the miasma.

The only alternative, however, was to cut back to the road, which, by now, was sure to be watched. We elected therefore to risk the ford, and found the water did not rise above the axles of our carriage, although the smell was rather pronounced, and the clouds of biting insects were a nuisance.

In this way we carried on for I forget how many days, being passed on from one band of charcoal burners to another as we progressed, until we found ourselves led out onto the open road again by our latest pathfinder, a particularly unprepossessing individual who had had nothing but scowls for us all the way from his camp.

"Napoles," he grunted, pointing south.

"E sicura, la via?" asked Charles, "Non ci sono soldati Francesi?"

"Cos'e la sicurezza?" was the reply, "Ci sono soldati ovunque, ma qui, sono Napoletani. Ora devo andare. Addio."

And with that we were abandoned in sight, we hoped, of our goal.

Of course, the inevitable happened. Mounting the crest of the first hill we came to, we could see, in the far distance, the gleam of a river which Charles pronounced to be the border of the Kingdom of the Two Sicilies, although I cannot help but think that this statement arose from wishful thinking quite as much as from any actual knowledge of the terrain. But then, just as we thought the end of our troubles was in sight, around the bend in the road behind us came the clattering, clinking sound of a troop of cavalry, followed shortly by their dust cloud and the horsemen themselves. They flew no flag or ensign, but their bright breastplates and horsehair crested helmets were unmistakeable.

"French cuirassiers!" cried Mr Thorpe, whipping out a long barreled pistol of obviously foreign origin.

In Rome, by the way, they have their own peculiar form of gun lock, which differs in some incomprehensible but highly significant way from the English lock, as both Charles and Mr Thorpe were at some pains to explain to me in a later moment of leisure. They might as well have saved their breath and their time, however, for I was none the wiser when they had finished.

Forgive me, my dear, but it occurred to me that

if Henry were reading this he would say that my narrative had gone on too long and literary convention required some divagatory passage by way of a distraction, or to build up the suspense.

I always try to give satisfaction, but I fear my talents do not lie in that direction, so I will get back to my tale.

"Put that away, you fool!" cried Charles. "Would you involve your sister and my lady in a fight with who knows how many French soldiers?"

"What shall we do?" cried Isabella, "They will catch us and shoot us for spies, I know they will."

"We shall keep our heads, and our dignity," replied Charles, "and keep calm. We are, after all, English. But first we shall make a few changes."

"Thorpe, inside with you. I shall drive for now. I shall stow my coat, tousle my hair, dirty my face and become the perfect Italian coachman. Miss Thorpe, wrap your brother up in your long, black cloak, and clap your most voluminous bonnet on his head. If they catch us, I shall spin them a tale of bringing my mistress and her two sisters back from her late husband's funeral. They are looking for two couples, not one man and three ladies, if they are looking for us at all, that is. Perhaps they will look no further."

"What if they insist on searching us?" I enquired.

"If they do that, we are lost, and a few popguns will not save us. But I will enlarge upon the morbid pestilence that carried my master off so quickly, and mention that I fear my mistress is already carrying the infection. Perhaps I shall add a cough or a groan or two of my own, and with any luck they will content themselves with merely glancing inside."

"But in any case I have a plan for avoiding the need for such a charade."

"Really?" I responded. "In that case do you have any objection to sharing it?"

"None whatsoever, my love. It is simply this. Now that we have completed our preparations, we shall, in a calm, dignified, English manner, run like billy-oh."

So we did, and a good thing it was that the horses were well-rested after so many days travel on foot. Otherwise they would never have carried us so quickly down the hill and along the road towards the bridge to safety. It was an even better thing that the French did not apparently notice us until they themselves had crested the hill. Then, of course, they could not miss our dust cloud, and the pursuit began in earnest.

They made good speed themselves, and were almost within carbine-shot when we sped across the bridge.

"Benvenuti al Regno 'e Napule," cried Charles. "We are safe now."

"Are you sure?" I replied, for our pursuers showed no sign of stopping, or even of slowing down.

Things must have gone badly with us, had we not rounded the next bend and spied a Customs Post, with a white flag bearing an elaborate coat of arms floating above it, and better still, a white-uniformed company of infantry in the road outside.

That, I must confess, is the sight I found even more welcome, at the time, than your letter, and I hope you will not begrudge my selfishness, given the circumstances.

Charles shouted something to their officer in heavily-accented Italian far too rapid for me to catch, whereupon that worthy individual ordered his men to fix bayonets and advance to meet the invaders.

Whatever the French officer's orders may have been, they evidently did not include starting another war just yet, and, with bad grace, the cavalry turned and went back the way they had come.

I will not weary you further, my pet, with an account of all the explanations and formalities that followed before we were escorted to Capua, whence we were eventually allowed to make our way onwards to Naples itself.

But I *will* invite you to join in our rejoicing that we are now once more in safety, for the time being, at least, and to sing a *Te Deum* for

Your much-chastened sister,

Eleanor

Letter the Thirty-Sixth :   Miss Morland to Lady Hapworth, in Naples

Fullerton

18th June 1803

Darling Eleanor,

How happy you have made me – indeed- how happy you have made us all with your latest! To know that you were safe has been our chiefest care, and your letter has lifted a great weight from our hearts.

But how like a novel of the most outlandish sort it has been to read! And how brave and resourceful your Charles must be! I should have been absolutely terrified into complete rigidity, that is to say, if I had not collapsed into a faint on first sight of the French. I shall never again consider the Black Veil the most horrid thing I have read.

Pray send no more of these dreadful tales. That is to say, please continue our correspondence, which has been one of my chief delights of the past months, but I beg you to take no more risks of a like nature. I will not ask you again to come home, for you must be weary beyond measure of such requests, but I fear that while you have those here who love you they will not cease altogether.

We have been very dull here by comparison. I continue to stock up my trousseau, and Henry continues to try to get his builders to come back and finish the work they have started, but nothing really exciting has, I think, ever happened around Fullerton, and even Northanger has only been the setting for skullduggery in the rather too vivid imagination of a certain young lady who longs to see you again and begs you to take great care of yourself and perhaps consider the possibility of returning to the arms of your family and the love of

Your anxious friend,

Catherine

Letter the Thirty-seventh : Lady Hapworth to Miss Morland

Naples

18th June 1803

Dearest Catherine,

Now that I have caught my breath and we have settled down into comfortable lodgings, I can be reasonable about describing this latest city to you.

Whoever coined the saying "*Vedere Napoli e poi morire*" had his justification, certainly. At the moment I am in love with Naples as a return to security and to civilization, and find myself disposed to overlook its teeming back streets and crumbling tenements, but even were I in the most critical mood I could not but marvel at the view across the bay to Vesuvius. The strictest devotees of the picturesque could not find in it anything at which to cavil.

We shall not be tarrying longer than we have to, however, for all its charms, and they are many.

Nostalgia in its true sense is creeping upon us.

Even Charles does not think that we shall stay here long. Our recent jaunt has given both of us our fill of foreign parts, and we are now looking forward to hastening a certain event which has been put off for far too long. We shall take the first ship which is going in the right direction, whether it be to England, or Spain, or even Malta. I will try to write to you before we leave, and let you know where to write next, or even, God willing, when to expect the arrival of

Your older and wiser friend,

Eleanor

Letter the Thirty-eighth :   Lady Hapworth to Miss Morland

Naples

18th June 1803

Dear Catherine,

We leave Naples tomorrow, and in leaving I regret nothing more than that I shall miss any last letter you may have sent here.

Charles has found us passage to Palermo, which is at least in the right direction, and should be as safe as anywhere in these troubled times. Even at the height of the last war, the French never reached Sicily, and I cannot conceive that the Royal Navy will allow them to do so now.

We are leaving after little more than a week in this fascinating city, so full of curiosities even after the passage of the plundering French army in the last war.

But it has been another busy week, I fear.

We have viewed the Roman remains at Pompeii; we have traversed the ancient tunnel to Posilippo, and marveled at Vergil's tomb. We have even ascended Vesuvius, and peered into the very depths of the volcano. The sight of the molten rock, glowing red in the dark interior was quite effecting, but I fear you would have liked neither the heat nor the smell. We have also trod the Phlegraean fields, and visited the Sybil's cave, Charles quoting, all the while, the relevant passages from the Aeneid. The English educational system certainly has a great deal to answer for.

We have lingered, too, as sunset kissed the waterfront at Chiaia, and heard the boatmen singing in the distance to attract their customers. Charles, who affects to understand the Neapolitan dialect, transcribed a verse, and I include it here as an example -

Comme se frícceca
la luna chiena!
lo mare ride,
ll'aria è serena...
È pronta e lesta
la varca mia...
Santa Lucia,

Santa Lucia!

When written down like that I can stumble my way through most of it, but I assure you that when spoken by the locals it is almost impenetrable.

As you are aware, my dear, I am not particularly given to romantic feelings, but I defy anyone – any female, certainly – to cross the Bay of Naples by moonlight with her lover, as the boatman sings softly to them and the night, and not be unaffected.

Perhaps you may have surmised that I have developed an affection for this city, and I suppose I have. But it is not all sweetness and light. There are areas of indescribable squalor, such as would make a London rookery look a desirable place of residence. Charles tells me that there are apartment blocks in the city which have been continuously occupied since Roman times, and I could well believe it.

But we have been happy here, and carefree for a short time. Perhaps it is a combination of relief after the perils of our flight from Rome and regret that our honeymoon is ending, but I shall be sorry to leave Naples.

I shall be far from sorry, however, to see you again, especially as that sight will very soon be followed by a certain very happy event.

Until then, think kindly of

Your rather complacent sister,

Eleanor.

Letter the Thirty-Ninth :   Miss Morland to Lady Hapworth, in Palermo

Fullerton

25th June 1803

Dear Eleanor,

How I do hope this finds you well, and safely in Palermo at last. I have never really understood why there should be a Kingdom of the Two Sicilies, when there is but one upon the map. I dare say the reason is quite clear when you are there, but I have never been able to make it out.

In your last letter, you seemed to regret the leaving of Naples so much that I cannot help but wonder whether I have been too selfish in prevailing upon you to start your return home before you were ready. Dearest Eleanor, pray take no heed of me when I am in my nervous fits. I know nothing of

Continental travel and its dangers, and very little of English travel, for that matter. What is my opinion when weighed against that of the brave, adventurous, knowledgeable, experienced traveller that you have become? And yet, Henry says that Bonaparte could march into Naples any day he chose, and the only thing the Neapolitan government could do about it is to take refuge in Sicily once more.

I am glad that you have preceded them. In Sicily, with the Royal Navy to protect you, you should be very nearly as safe as we are at home.

Write very soon, I beg you, and delight the heart of

Your loving sister,

Catherine

Letter the Fortieth : Miss Thorpe to Miss Morland

Palermo

1st July 1803

Dear, sweet Catherine,

I dare say you are quite surprised to get a letter from me. It seems such age since we met in Bath and had such fun together.

I am afraid I have some serious news to tell you. Viscountess Hapworth, Miss Tilney as was, my dear friend and yours, who has been good enough to acknowledge the utility of my assistance to her in the past few weeks, has been struck down with a fever.

The Viscountess has been very good to both of us. (Do you know that John is here too, by the way? He often speaks kindly of you, and I cannot help thinking there is still something of a *tendre* there.) and I know that she has been corresponding with you, for she often gives me letters to take to the post. I try to help her generally and make myself as useful as I can, for you know, my dear, that idleness is foreign to my nature.

The poor lady lies abed as I write, tossing, turning and moaning, quite delirious I fear. I have sent after Lord Hapworth, who has chosen this day of all days to absent himself from the city. I believe he has gone to Marsala to enquire if there is any chance of a ship to England from that port. Meanwhile, the Italian physician from round the corner is absolutely useless, and cannot be made to understand what is wanted.

I will write again as soon as I have more news, but in the mean time, I fear very greatly for my patroness, and thought I ought to inform you so that you might prepare the family for an unfavourable outcome.

We all hope it will not come to that, naturally, and you may rest assured that the poor, suffering invalid will receive every care and attention that can possibly be given from the capable and reliable hands of

Your old friend

Isabella Thorpe

Letter the Forty-First : Miss Morland to Miss Thorpe, in Palermo

Fullerton

8th July 1803

Dear Miss Thorpe,

Thank you for your letter informing me of your employer's indisposition.

I am, naturally concerned to hear this news, and shall write personally to His Lordship with my condolences and a request for a full report on my friend's condition.

For your good wishes and service I am obliged to you.

Catherine Morland

Letter the Forty-Second : Miss Morland to Viscount Hapworth, in Palermo

Fullerton

8th July 1803

My lord,

Miss Thorpe has been so good as to inform me of your wife's illness, which has caused me great concern. Although we have never met, you must be aware that Lady Hapworth and I were the greatest of friends when she was still Miss Tilney, and that we have been corresponding during her absence on the continent.

I should be very sorry should any great harm befall her, and I beg you to set my mind at ease, if that may be, or else reveal the worst.

You must be aware that I am a very timorous creature, much given to taking alarm, and I should be very happy to learn that my fears – much heightened by Miss Thorpe's communication - have been groundless. Lady Hapworth has always urged me to be more optimistic in my outlook, and in that spirit I enclose a note to her, which I entreat you to pass on should the state of her health permit.

In doing so you will greatly oblige

Your humble servant

Catherine Morland.

Letter the Forty-Third :   Miss Morland to Lady Hapworth, in Palermo

Fullerton

8th July 1803

Dear, dear Eleanor,

What a shock it was to me to hear that you are not well! And to hear it from Isabella Thorpe, too! She may not be quite the last person I should choose to attend the sick bed of any person I love, but she is a very long way from the first.

I think it was very remiss of your husband to leave you with only those two – I will not quite say "rascals", but I think you will know what I mean – for company, even if it was with the intention of finding a quicker passage home.

I have always thought that foreign parts were, by their nature, unhealthy, and have often marvelled at the robustness of your constitution, my darling, which has enabled you to survive them for so long.

I pray that your indisposition may only be of a mild nature, and soon past, and long to have it confirmed to me. Write soon, I beg you, or cause someone whose account I may credit to write for you, and ease the suspense of

Your anxious friend,

Catherine.

Letter the Forty-Fourth : Lord Hapworth to Miss Morland

Palermo
15th July 1803

My Dear Catherine,

I, in my turn, must beg you to be less formal in any future address. You are my wife's dear friend and shortly to be her sister, are you not? I know that dear Eleanor refers to me in her letter to you as Charles, and I wish that you would do so also.

As for Eleanor's health, she was a little indisposed but now is quite recovered, and I will let her tell you all the details herself.

We hope to be home before the month is out, and are looking forward with great anticipation to a happy event which I believe is due to take place shortly thereafter.

Until then, believe me to be,

Your affectionate friend,

Charles

**Letter the Forty-Fifth :   Lady Hapworth
to Miss Morland**

Palermo

15th July 1803

Dear, dear Catherine,

Pray do not distress yourself. The rumours of my demise have been greatly exaggerated. It was, literally, nothing to write home about, merely a touch of fever, picked up, no doubt in the marshes on our flight from Rome. The Peruvian Bark in Charles's medicine chest set it right almost immediately.

Isabella's letter I see as an attempt to establish herself in your good graces again. Already, it appears, she is considering how she is to continue when we return to England, which is just as well, for I shall certainly have no further use for her there.

I am up and about now, and going around Palermo like any tourist. We arrived with the dawn, and should have been able to see the city at the best advantage. The harbour, however, is long and narrow, much like Marseilles in shape and size, but rather less impressive, being low-lying and surrounded by warehouses and suchlike buildings rather than by towering fortresses.

By far its most impressive sight when we arrived was the three ships of war moored alongside, flying the White Ensign from their masts. There is something terribly reassuring about such a spectacle. It brings to mind Lord St Vincent's comment, when asked whether the French would invade England.

"I do not say they cannot come" he replied. "I only say they cannot come by sea."

What a comfort it is to be on an island again!

We are staying at the palace of the Prince of Salina. This sounds very grand, and is, to a degree, but princes in Sicily are even thicker on the ground than they are in Rome, and many of them make no bones about hiring off surplus accommodation. In fact, almost everyone one encounters in Sicily seems to have a title of some sort. Charles tell me that most of them are self-bestowed, that there is even a proverb about them – "*Ognuno e Conte di Nulla.*"

There is another English party here, the Dowager Lady Dalrymple and her daughter, the Honourable Miss Carteret. The mother is recently widowed, of a certain age, and quite polite enough to pass in society for "charming". It is a great source of amusement to see the way Isabella attempts to ingratiate herself with both ladies, and the way they both accept her adulation as if the pudding could not possibly be over-egged.

Lady Dalrymple has been in Sicily to liquidate her late husband's interest in the Marsala wine trade, having herself nothing against the wine, but much against the fell word "trade." She has not demeaned herself to such an extent as to visit the wineries in person, still less the vineyards, but her visit has been so far successful that she has a chestful of gold ducats to take back to England with her, being wary of foreign letters of credit. Like us, she is waiting for a passage home, of which there is no sign yet, I fear.

Unlike the other Italian cities on our tour, Palermo benefits from never having suffered the depredations of a French army, thanks, of course, to Lord Nelson and other ships like those at present in port. The city is nowhere near so picturesque as Naples, but has its attractions. At last Charles has had the pleasure of seeing a Caravaggio in the setting for which it was painted, the Nativity in the Church of St. Lazarus.

Many of the other sights are quite strange, both to our eyes and those of most mainland Italians.

One of them, indeed, would just suit you, with your love of the horrid and romantic. The Catacombe dei Cappucini would satisfy the worst nightmares of the most Gothickally addicted. These endless underground corridors are filled with the mummified bodies of Palermitans of bygone days, not laid out in tombs or coffins, but hanging on the walls, arranged in lifelike poses, grinning and glaring at the visitor as if about to come back to life and do whatever horrid things revivified mummies do. Originally these were all monks, but it has become the fashion to have oneself – or at least one's relatives – displayed here after death, and for those they have left behind to visit them regularly. It is not the sort of horror that would make me shriek out loud at first sight – although I would not answer for you, my dear - but the sense of creeping dread that slowly overpowers one as one walks past these rows and rows of those who have gone before is quite oppressive. Even Charles seemed not his usual self when we came out.

I wish we never had gone.

The cathedral is a great, Gothick pile, quite unlike most that one sees in Italy, made more singular still by having had a baroque dome clapped upon the crossing some time in the last age. Inside it, one may view the tombs of the Norman Kings, and very fine they are, too. Finer still, however, are the mosaics with which the walls are inlaid, done by Greeks from Constantinople when there was still an emperor there, at the behest of one of the Norman monarchs. The great figure of Christ under the apse, gazing sternly down – I almost said glaring – at the congregation while stretching out his arms to enfold them, is particularly impressive.

Strangest of all is the fact that it was designed by an Englishman, who was archbishop at the time, Walter of the Mill, or Gualtiero Offamiglio as they call him here. Norman kings, Royal Navy ships and English Archbishops. It all sounds very like a sort of muddled England.

But it does not look, or feel at all like England. The noise and the heat are quite different. What we think of as a hot summer's day in England is but a mild spring in Sicily. The streets are full of people of all degrees, and the markets require a shoe horn to effect access. And everywhere there are trees and flowers. Do you know Goethe's verse "*Kennst du das Land, wo die Zitronen blühn?*"? Well, here in Palermo, both oranges and lemons grow on trees, and litter the streets when they fall, unheeded from the boughs. The perfume of their blossoms fills the air, for both fruit and flower are borne at the same time. The effect is overpowering to a native of a northern clime.

But I fear I am waxing enthusiastic, and that will never do.

Nor will it do to become too fond of this temporary resting place on our journey home. The very first ship heading in the right direction will find us among its passengers, and what I really look forward to is seeing you again, and Henry, and planning the day when we shall truly be sisters.

Until then, have no fear, for you are always in the thoughts of

Your disgustingly healthy friend,

Eleanor.

Letter the Forty-Sixth : Miss Morland to Lady Hapworth, in Palermo

Fullerton

23rd July 1803

Dear, Dear Eleanor,

What a relief it was to get your letter, and to know that you are well and on your way home. I am quite sure, now that I consider, that that wicked Isabella was practising upon me, hoping to insinuate herself back into my affections. If so, her subterfuge has had quite the opposite effect to the one she desired, for I shall never credit anything I hear from her lips, or read from her hand, again.

You make Sicily sound almost like paradise on earth, which I am sure I had never thought that it might be. One hears so many tales about banditti, and robber barons and so forth. But perhaps I am falling back into my old habits, and Sicilian Barons are no worse than English ones, except that you tell me that most of them have no right to their titles in the first place.

My father and Henry both tell me that everything that can be done by way of preparation for Henry's and my wedding has been done, and there only remains a day to name. Sally is becoming urgent for her chance to wear her bridesmaid's dress, and even worse to relate, Henry is pressing me to name a date without waiting for your return.

He has been so patient, waiting all this while, that I am hard pressed to refuse, but it will not be at all the same without you.

I have always been careful not to lay any demands upon you, but now that you are on your way home in any case, I feel myself justified in saying –

Come home soon, my darling, and make complete the bridal day of

Your loving friend,

Catherine.

Letter the Forty-Seventh : Lady Hapworth to Miss Morland

Gibraltar

1st August 1803

Dear Catherine,

We are but newly arrived in Gibraltar, which can best be described as a sort of Spanish Portsmouth with a great rock at one end of the single street, towering over everything. We had hoped to transfer straight to an Indiaman bound for London, but we arrived, it seems, too late, and another is not expected for a month yet.

This has greatly discomposed Lady Dalrymple, who had counted on the *Lord Mornington* to take her home. Now that she is stranded in this excessively naval environment without even servants of her own, she was quite at a loss what to do, until I suggested that she engage the Thorpes to perform for her similar services to those they had been performing for us these past few months.

Isabella had already taken pains to win her way into Lady Dalrymple's confidence, and this new arrangement was pronounced capital by all involved.

I wish them joy of each other, and cannot describe to you the relief that I feel that I shall not feel obliged to carry them back with me as unwelcome guests at a certain ceremony.

I am relieved, also, that we shall not have to spend another month in their company. There is a trading vessel leaving tomorrow for Bristol, with a cargo of sherry from the vineyards just across the border, and we have persuaded her master to carry us home. The accommodations may be less prepossessing then than those of John Company but the advantage of docking at Bristol, a mere step away from you all, compared to London, more than makes up for the discomfort.

In fact, we are very lucky to come upon this ship. The sherry boats sail from San Lucar de Barrameda, in Spain, and avoid Gibraltar if they can help it, for fear of losing men to the Press. This one was driven to take shelter from a storm a week ago, and is already late in its voyage. The master proposes therefore to press on, in the hope of making up for lost time.

I fear we shall be carrying back very little in the way of souvenirs. The paintings and *pietra dura* and micromosaics and china were all lost when we had to flee Rome, but we have a few little things for everyone to pretend delight over, and I have carefully preserved the Parisian gown for you through all our vicissitudes.

See how we can press on when once we have decided to follow your very excellent advice, my dear.

The mariners assure us that we should be in Bristol within the week, and I must therefore bid you steel yourself for the arrival of

Your wandering sister,

Eleanor

Letter the Forty-Eighth :   Mr Henry Tilney to Lady Hapworth, at Bristol

Woodston

7th August 1803

Dear Eleanor,

I am addressing this to you aboard ship at Bristol, and sending it specially by a trusted servant to make sure it reaches you.

If at all possible, please come directly to Woodston, so that we may go on together to Fullerton, where we shall have the ceremony the day after your arrival. The banns have all been called, Catherine's father stands ready to officiate, and James to give her away, so why should we delay further?

Catherine was at first reluctant to accept my proposal that we should delay no longer, as she had set her heart on having you as her matron of honour. But, however, she was eventually persuaded that I was constitutionally incapable of waiting any longer, and gave her consent. It is remarkable how much a good fit of the sulks will work upon her.

She still does not know of your arrival (you see, I am taking it, and you, for granted as usual), and I plan it to be a surprise.

Do not worry about wedding clothes. They are all arranged. Do you not have a brother here who both knows your measurements and understands muslin?

Have no care for wedding presents either. What better gift could you give us than your return from all your adventures?

Just come, do come, please come, and make complete the happiness of

Your ridiculously selfish brother,

Henry.

Letter the Forty-Ninth : Mrs Henry Tilney to Captain Tilney

Woodston

7th August 1803

Mrs Henry Tilney presents her compliments to Captain Tilney, and encloses a slice of wedding cake, with the sincerest expressions of her regret that the requirements of the service prevented his attendance at her marriage to his brother.

She also wishes Captain Tilney to understand that she looks forward to welcoming him to her new home at his earliest convenience.

Letter the Fiftieth :   Lady Hapworth to Captain Tilney

Northanger Monachorum

8th August 1803

Dear Frederick,

I am enclosing a card from our new sister, with the necessary piece of cake, to inform you of the success of the ceremony yesterday.

I am perfectly familiar with your self-centred nature, and have no doubt that you would be content to let matters rest at that and hear no more.

But it will not do. I will not let it do. Catherine is undoubtedly a member of our family now, and you ought to hear of her happiness, and you shall, whether it suits you or not.

Charles and I had come straight from the docks at Bristol, where we had been met on arrival from Gibraltar by Henry's servant and conveyed directly to Woodston.

Henry had some scheme in mind of surprising his bride with my presence, of which she had despaired.

"I cannot wait to see the look on her face tomorrow," he said, "when she starts lamenting your absence, which I am sure she will, and I tell her I have a surprise for her, open the door, and you walk in, Eleanor. Will it not be a perfect sell?"

"Will it not be rather unkind to your bride?" I replied. "That is the question you should be asking."

"You do not think, then, that the surprise will heighten the pleasure more than enough to make up for the preliminary deception?"

"I do not. And, in any case, I do not see how the look on her face when I arrive could be visible to you."

"How so? What do you mean?"

"Have you forgotten that it is your wedding morning? You are not to see the bride until you meet in church. Would you have your marriage start off on such an unlucky footing?"

"Oh, stuff! Does anyone still take notice of that

old fancy?"

"I think you will not find a female within a hundred miles who does not, and that includes Miss Catherine Morland. I shall go to her now."

"It is far too late to be making the journey now, on top of the drive from Bristol. You will be quite fagged out. No, we shall all go in the morning, and I shall peep through the crack in the door to see her face when she greets you."

"No, you shall not. That would be quite as bad as walking in upon her. I am not quite sure that it would not be worse."

You know what your brother is like when he gets an idea into his head, but you also know what your sister is like.

Eventually we settled that we might go together to Fullerton in the morning, and that I should go in to Catherine as she was dressing, and that Henry was to content himself with listening below the window, Charles being instructed to make sure he did no more. Henry was then to go directly to the church before anyone left the house.

I will not trouble you with a relation of my

meeting with Catherine again. Such a thing would only bore you and embarrass me.

I am almost tempted to cry fie upon you, Frederick, but I am still in the mood to be joyful, both at my return home and at yesterday's happy event, so I will give you the benefit of the doubt and believe that the sudden selection of the date took you unawares, rather than that you forgot your own brother's wedding, at which you had such an important part to play.

But you may rest assured that the wedding was all that such things might be wished to be, and that your absence made not the slightest difference to the happiness of anyone concerned.

Charles made a far better best man than you would ever have managed, and my new sister Sally was a beautiful bridesmaid, and much admired by all the guests.

The bride was absolutely adorable, and looked completely ravishing in her bridal gown, even if the muslin had been selected by the groom. My own dress, by the way, chosen by the same person, was markedly inferior, even after I had sat up half the night making a few, necessary alterations. A gentleman may understand muslin well enough, but a lady likes to be consulted in the cut and design of her gowns.

Even our father unbent far enough to compliment Mr Morland on the way he had conducted the service, and Mrs Morland on her china. I believe he even wished young Sally well in her endeavours to be next.

The happy couple are gone to Derbyshire for their honeymoon, and have engaged lodgings in the town of Lambton. There are, I believe, many noteworthy sights in the neighbourhood, and at least one great house which may be visited. Catherine, of course, would not hear of a continental trip in the present state of affairs, and you know Henry's feelings about broad.

So now you may go off to the wars in the comfortable knowledge that the "little mouse" you so despised at Bath last year, and whose friend you used so heartlessly, is now your sister, and, what is more, she actually means all the conventional sentiments on the enclosed card.

Open sincerity is something of a novelty to the Tilney family, but it is one virtue that is sometimes rewarded, and not only in Gothick novels.

And with that in mind, dear Frederick, be ever sure of the best wishes of your devoted sister,

Eleanor.

THE END.

Lightning Source UK Ltd.
Milton Keynes UK
UKOW04n1534241017
311574UK00003B/33/P